TROUBLE IN PARADISE

There were no clouds on Lisa Meredith's horizon when she approached the Caribbean island of Santa Angelina for a reunion with her father. But bad news greeted her and she realised that Santa Angelina, with its poverty and squalor, was no island paradise . . . More disturbing was the attitude towards Lisa of those around her, and of Dr. Miguel Rodriguez. Amid seething undercurrents of an island on the brink of revolution, Lisa was drawn into a vortex of love and danger.

30
AC

GEORGINA FERRAND

◆

TROUBLE IN PARADISE

Complete and Unabridged

LINFORD
Leicester

First published in Great Britain in 1972 by
Robert Hale Limited
London

First Linford Edition
published 2006
by arrangement with
Robert Hale Limited
London

British Library CIP Data

Ferrand, Georgina
Trouble in paradise.—Large print ed.—
Linford romance library
1. Love stories
2. Large type books
I. Title
823.9'14 [F]

ISBN 1–84617–300–0

Published by
F. A. Thorpe (Publishing)
Anstey, Leicestershire

Set by Words & Graphics Ltd.
Anstey, Leicestershire
Printed and bound in Great Britain by
T. J. International Ltd., Padstow, Cornwall

This book is printed on acid-free paper

1

As *The Master of Kentucky* cleaved a snowy-white path through a cobalt sea Lisa leaned over the rail, her eyes alight with suppressed excitement. A gentle breeze tempered the heat and ruffled her shoulder length corn-coloured hair. She raised one hand to wave to the brown-skinned crew of a schooner, who stood on its deck silently watching as the tanker cut across its bow.

At the sound of footsteps behind her she turned. 'Not long now Captain,' she said with a gay laugh.

'Two more hours Miss Meredith,' he replied. 'Two more hours before we dock at Alhaja de mar.'

Lisa brushed back her hair with her hands and regarded the tanned, weather-beaten face that had seen countless years at sea. 'You can't imagine how long I've waited for this day.'

1

Captain Tregear moved over to stand by her side, his hands linked on top of the rail. His eyes were narrowed as he peered into the distance. 'I hope you're not disappointed Miss Meredith. I really hope so. These islands look very pretty in the travel brochures but in reality they're often quite primitive. Not that Santa Angelina is a tourist trap; it's a little off the so-called 'holiday route'.'

Lisa laughed again. 'That's quite all right Captain, I'm well aware of the island's shortcomings. My excitement, I assure you, is due entirely to the prospect of seeing my father again. It's been six years and then for only a month during the school holidays. It's my chance to get to know him at last.'

Captain Tregear smiled at her, thinking to himself that she was a very engaging girl and her father was a lucky man. For once he had not resented the presence of a passenger on his ship despite the fact that she was pretty enough to divert his crew's attention from its job. At first he had considered her to be nothing more than a spoilt child on whom money had been lavished in default of parental affection and discipline. As the days at sea passed he had realised his initial judgement was ill-founded; there was something both innocent and beguiling in those clear grey eyes. Now his resentment had passed on to the unseen father who after providing his daughter with a lifetime of comfort and civilised living caused her to cross the Atlantic to join him on such a backward island as Santa Angelina. Despite her protestations to the contrary he was sure she was eagerly anticipating days of bathing and basking in the sun on an island paradise. But as she was so enthusiastic he hesitated to disillusion her. Not that it was his place to do so; she was just another passenger after all, even if she was more attractive than most.

'In that case,' he said aloud, 'I shall wish you luck. Providing you don't expect too much you'll enjoy yourself. You'll be staying in Alahaja de mar; it's safe enough there by all accounts.'

Lisa's confident, and slightly dreamy smile, faded slightly. 'Safe? What do you mean by safe?'

'Only that there's been some rumour of revolution in the offing. I don't think it's anything serious — I don't suppose for one moment your father would have sent for you if it was. President Pantero keeps everything under his personal control and so far all trouble has been contained in the hill areas.' He stole a glance at her. 'Don't you worry Miss Meredith; revolution and counter revolution are everyday occurrences in this part of the world.'

Lisa's smile returned to her face. 'Being British it all sounds very dramatic, but it's odd my father never mentioned it in his letters. You must be right when you say it can't be serious.'

'At the moment there's nothing to indicate they're anything more than a bunch of roughnecks. The trouble is information coming from Santa Angelina is never very regular or reliable. My men get all their information from the dockside cantinas and it's only gossip at that.' He turned briskly. 'You'll have me turning the ship around and heading back to New York if I go on like this.'

'Oh no I won't!' She rubbed her arm ruefully. 'If having all those jabs didn't frighten me off nothing will!'

'You've got pluck enough to be a sailor's wife, Miss Meredith. Will you excuse me? I have some paper work to do before we dock.'

Lisa fell into step behind him. 'I'd better finish my packing. I want to be back on deck in plenty of time to get my first sight of land the moment it appears. Flying may be quicker and more convenient but you can't beat sailing for the view.'

'You'd have a hard job flying to this island Miss Meredith — there's no airport.'

Lisa stopped short and looked up at him, her eyes sparkling mischievously, 'I shall be most disappointed if you don't warn me about hurricanes Captain.'

His lips twitched into an involuntary smile. 'Well I *am* sorry to disappoint you, but you see Santa Angelina is just out of the hurricane belt and the island, I believe, hasn't been hit by one for more than a hundred years.'

Her excitement knew no bounds as the ancient tanker steered a direct course to Alhaja de mar. The island, at first no bigger than a speck on the horizon, gradually took form in front of her eyes. For Lisa *The Master of Kentucky*, steamed far too slowly to its destination but there was nothing she could do about that except stand impatiently on deck, her eyes fixed almost feverishly on the place she would, in future, call home. A few miles out from land the tanker was joined by two gun boats that escorted it into port.

She had expected the island to be beautiful and as the tanker approached the port she found her enthusiasm ebbing slightly. True she could see countless palm trees but from where she stood there appeared to be no beaches. A mass of green cloaked hills merging with a cloudless sky provided a backdrop for the harbour and the buildings edging the wharf. And higher up on a hill a grey stone fortress stood stark against the sky, its now useless cannons staring out to sea like sightless eyes.

From a distance the buildings along the wharf appeared picturesque with their red shingle roofs contrasting with white clapboard façades and the inevitable balconies arcading the street below from the incessant tropical sun. But as she neared her destination the peeling paintwork became all too apparent and the balconies dipped precariously from lack of support.

Lisa leaned over the side straining to catch sight of her father. The wharf was so crowded with colourfully clad people whose skins varied in hue between the lightest olive to the darkest ebony she couldn't hope to spot him. Her nostrils immediately detected the unwholesome smell of fruit rotting in the sun and rubbish that had been tipped into the sea.

The arrival of the tanker seemed to be quite an event for the islanders. They crowded forward smiling broadly. A statuesque negress strolled along, a huge basket of oranges perfectly balanced on her head, and squatting beneath one of the verandas a coconut seller attempted to ply his trade. A young boy dressed in rags begged from the more prosperous-looking people, only to be rudely repulsed by each in turn.

As she waited with scarcely concealed impatience for the gangway to be lowered Lisa watched in fascination the teeming life on the wharf. It was as though the whole island's activities was suddenly centred around her.

A crowd began to gather where two dusky-skinned women were arguing over the ownership of a red skirt. Suddenly the argument erupted into violence as one woman slapped the other and in a second the two were sprawling on the ground, much to the delight of the crowd.

Lisa's attention was suddenly diverted from the unusual spectacle by a black limousine inching its way along the wharf. Its horn being blasted continuously failed to scatter the ambling islanders who ignored its presence until they were almost knocked down by the vehicle.

This she was sure must be her father arriving and she hurried to where the gangway had been lowered to the wharf below.

Captain Tregear was waiting at the top of the gangway. 'Well,' he said smilingly, 'you're here at last. I hope you have a very happy stay. Your bags have just been taken ashore.'

'Thank you Captain,' she said extending her hand, 'And thank you for a very pleasant journey.'

'But not quite speedy enough,' he added with a laugh.

The black limousine was now parked at the foot of the gangway and as Lisa stared down she experienced a stab of disappointment at not seeing her father waiting there. She started down with one last wave to Captain Tregear and several of his crew who had wanted to say goodbye to her. When she was halfway down she noticed the occupant of the car standing by its side. He was a stocky young man of middle height, surprisingly light-skinned and fair-haired. He was standing stiffly to attention and wore a khaki uniform relieved by scarlet epaulettes and he held his cap — similarly flashed with scarlet — under one arm. As she descended slowly she noticed he was studying her intently but his face remained completely expressionless so that she couldn't tell what impression she was making on him.

Her spirits flagged slightly when she realised her father was not, after all, meeting her from the boat; he had obviously sent this man instead.

When she reached the wharf he hurried forward, bowing stiffly. 'Señorita Meredith?'

Her eyes travelled involuntarily to the leather holster strapped around his waist and the pistol it contained. 'Yes, I was expecting my father — Major Meredith.'

The young man's lips curved into a reluctant smile. 'I am Luis Baldera — Captain of The President's Personal Guard. His excellency's car is at your disposal.'

For a second or two Lisa digested the information. Now she noticed the gold and blue flag fluttering from the bonnet of the car and felt a little thrill because her father must be important enough to merit the use of the president's own limousine. Her mind also registered the fact that the babble of noise on the wharf had died down considerably and even the two women had stopped their fight and were now regarding Lisa and Captain Baldera with curious and slightly hostile expressions.

Captain Baldera touched her arm lightly, 'Please señorita, we must leave now.'

Another man — also in a khaki uniform flashed with red — jumped forward to open the door of the limousine. Lisa climbed into the back followed by Captain Baldera.

As the driver began to edge the car backwards off the wharf Lisa stared out at the countless brown faces looking in at her. She turned to the young man at her side, a dozen questions on her lips, but at the sight of his face staring woodenly ahead, she bit them back and settled into her seat instead.

Once clear of the harbour the car climbed upwards through narrow cobbled streets bounded by tall houses. The car passed under lines of grubby washing strung across from balcony to balcony. Eventually they came into a wider street flanked by shops selling every kind of merchandise imaginable, their fronts open onto stone arcades. All around people teemed into the road, staring expressionlessly at the big car as it passed. So slow was their progress because of unhurried pedestrians Lisa had a chance to take stock of her

surroundings which were more diladi-
pated than she would ever have
imagined possible.

This street appears to be the main
shopping centre, she thought with
dismay. It opened into a large cobbled
square and this was obviously the older
part of the town. When they emerged
from the shopping street there were two
directions in which they could go
— straight ahead into the square itself
or up another steeply narrow road
which she saw led to the fortress. When
she peered up at it through the window
of the car Lisa could hardly repress a
shudder. It looked much larger and far
more grim than it had from the boat. To
her relief the car surged ahead into the
square itself.

A high stone wall ran along both
sides of the square and each wall had a
tall double gate in the centre of it. At
the top of the square stood an old
church with twin domes, its ancient
stonework peeling sadly from centuries
of neglect and erosion.

In the middle of the square the car came to a standstill, a crowd of people pressed close staring expressionlessly into the interior, and although Lisa managed a half-hearted smile Luis Baldera still stared ahead taking no notice whatsoever of the clamour outside. The driver leaned over his already overworked horn and the gates swung open a few seconds later.

She strained forward eagerly. 'What is this place?'

'His Excellency's residence,' Captain Baldera replied importantly.

'And the other building across the square? The one with the wall around it too.'

'That is the Convent of Madre Mia. This is La Plaza de los Conquistadores.'

The car swept into a courtyard and stopped in front of a large and imposing stuccoed house. The driver jumped out smartly and opened the door. Captain Baldera stepped out first and offered his hand to her while the driver stood stiffly to attention holding open the door with one hand, saluting with the other.

Lisa hesitated to get out. She had come to Santa Angelina simply to join her father who was adviser to the president's army. She had hardly expected to be met by such an important personage as the Captain of The President's Personal Guard. In other circumstances she might have been amused by treatment more suited to visiting royalty but after looking forward to joining her father and journeying so far she was irritated by Captain Baldera's autocratic manner and the lack of communication between them.

Captain Baldera put his head inside the car. 'Please señorita,' he insisted.

She allowed him to hand her out of the car but when she straightened up she said stiffly, 'Is my father here Captain Baldera?'

He looked towards the door to the house, which was flanked by sentries, and then back to Lisa. 'His Excellency wishes to welcome you personally,' he said, not unkindly.

Lisa relaxed, satisfied. Her father, she knew, held an important position in the army and she was touched by the president's gesture. She smiled and he looked visibly relieved.

The thick wooden door was opened by one of the sentries and Lisa preceded Captain Baldera into a wide hall. The dimness after the light outside blinded her for a moment or two. She blinked and saw a large double staircase with a curled iron balustrade snaking its way upwards, each side of the staircase meeting as a balcony on the upper floor.

Captain Baldera's boots clicked on the cool tiled floor as he walked briskly towards the nearest branch of the staircase. He turned briefly to Lisa who was waiting just inside the door, her eyes taking in every detail. As she grew more accustomed to the interior of the house she noticed the presence of several armed guards, both downstairs and on the balcony above.

'This way Señorita Meredith.'

Hesitantly Lisa followed him up the marble stairs, conscious of their footsteps making hollow sounds which echoed off the harsh white walls and around the high ceiling. The guards made no acknowledgement of their presence; they just stared as woodenly into space as lead soldiers, but Lisa guessed they would spring sharply into action if the house or any of its inhabitants were threatened.

She followed her escort along seemingly endless corridors, many adorned with dismal paintings of soldiers of old or dusty tapestries. There were many shadowy alcoves sheltering bronze statuettes and busts.

As Captain Baldera paused in front of one of the doors leading off the corridor — also guarded by a soldier — she realised awsomely that she was about to come face to face with the president of Santa Angelina.

Her heart hammered painfully as her

escort knocked sharply at the door. At the sound of a peremptory *'Adalante!'* he opened it and Lisa passed into the room.

Sun streamed in from a window only partially shuttered. The walls were lined with books and the floor — tiled like the rest of the house — was partially covered with a faded carpet. The room was dominated by a large mahogany desk, richly polished and ornately carved.

The man sitting behind the desk raised his head as she entered and when the door closed behind her it came as a shock to her to realise the Captain had not accompanied her inside.

Strangely Lisa was disappointed that President Jorge Pantero looked a very ordinary man. He was below middle height — as she had noticed most Spaniards were — and tending to portliness. His hair was sparse and plastered across his head in an effort to make as much use as possible of what was left. But it was his eyes that caught

Lisa's attention; they were unbelievably shrewd and assessing.

He rose from his chair and hustled forward, extending both hands. 'My dear Miss Meredith. I am honoured to meet you.'

'And I'm overwhelmed at the extent of my welcome,' she replied, managing to release her hands from his clammy grasp. He did not wear the uniform of a soldier but a shabby and crumpled lightweight suit.

President Pantero ushered her to a chair. 'You must have refreshment.' He went over to a table bearing several bottles and decanters. 'You have come a very long way to our little island.

'It is worth it,' she replied as she accepted a tall glass of lime juice. She sipped it tentatively, wishing there was some ice available, but not daring to ask for some. Lisa was aware that the president was watching her carefully and she was beginning to be a little uneasy about the way she had been greeted. Surely she didn't merit such grand treatment as a personal greeting by the president himself.

'Your father has told me a great deal about you Miss Meredith — may I call you Lisa? I feel I know you so well already.'

'It would be less formal,' she replied warily.

'Then I shall call you Lisa.'

There was a short pause and then she said casually, hoping not to offend him. 'I was surprised my father didn't meet me himself, or at least have me taken directly to his own house.'

The president perched on the edge of his desk near to where she was sitting. 'Your father lived here.'

At the tone of his voice she looked up at him sharply, fear suddenly stabbing at her heart. 'Lived?'

President Pantero drew a deep sigh. 'I am afraid my dear,' he said gently, 'I have bad news for you. Your father is dead.'

For a moment she was stunned into silence and then she cried. 'Oh no! It can't be! It can't.'

The president removed the half empty glass from her hand and she buried her head in her hands. 'Cry my dear, if it will help.'

She shook her head as she looked up at him. It was too soon — too sudden — for tears. 'When did it happen? He was always so fit and healthy.'

He moved away from the desk and went across to the window, staring out. 'So he was. Your father was killed in the service of his country.' He turned to face her. 'The men concerned will hang in la plaza for all to see! This I promise you.'

Lisa stared at him wide-eyed with disbelief. 'He was murdered?'

'Yes it was no less than murder my dear.' He sat down at his desk and faced her across its expanse. 'We have had some trouble of late from a group of men who like to call themselves revolutionaries. They have had little success mainly because your father has trained our army so well. Last week he took a battery of men into the hills on training manoeuvres and they were ambushed by these barbarians who dare to call themselves patriots!'

'I can hardly believe it,' she said softly. It had all happened so swiftly, so unexpectedly. It seemed such a short time ago when she had excitedly anticipated her reunion with her father, and now it would never happen. She drew a handkerchief out of her bag and blew her nose. 'You've been very kind Your Excellency. I won't impose upon your hospitality any further.' She began to get up. 'There will be plenty of time for me to return on *The Master of Kentucky*.'

He smiled at her kindly. 'Please sit down for a little longer. You have come such a long way.' Lisa obeyed. She was so miserable she would have agreed to anything at that moment. 'Your mother is dead too I believe?' he asked.

'When I was fifteen,' she replied. Her mind went back to her frail mother who on Lisa's birth decided to stay in

England rather than share any longer the rigors of army life with her husband. Frank Meredith being unable to compromise stayed with the army, returning home only periodically to see his wife and daughter.

'Have you any other relatives in England?'

She nodded. 'I have aunts and uncles but I'm well able to take care of myself. My father believed that women should be self-supporting and he insisted I train for a job before I joined him. I have a certificate that enables me to teach.'

President Pantero nodded. 'He was a wise man. He talked to me often about you and he was looking forward to having you here with him.'

'I was looking forward to it too,' she replied miserably.

He shifted in his chair and cleared his throat noisily. 'I wonder if you would do me the honour,' he said, 'of staying here as my guest?'

She was startled. 'I couldn't,' she

stammered after a while. 'It's very kind of you . . . you've been more than kind already.'

'I am not being kind my dear. Major Meredith was not only a good friend to me but a loyal servant of my country. I feel it only right that I should take care of his daughter now he is dead. As his dependant you are entitled to a pension so you will not lack for money in the meantime. Let me make amends for his death in a small part by taking care of you, at least for a while until you feel more like returning to your own country. Take time to get to know the country your father learned to love.'

The prospect of returning across the Atlantic to the cold drizzly spring she thought she had left behind for good was not inviting. 'You put it very nicely Your Excellency,' she said after a moment's consideration. Staying until the next boat left could do no harm and she did want to see more of the island. 'I accept — very gratefully.'

Lisa stared out of the window of the bedroom she had been shown into by a maid who could not speak English. Night had come quickly. She had been told her room overlooked the garden but apart from the fragrant scent that floated upwards to invade her numbed senses and the fireflies glowing out of the darkness there was no way of knowing.

The maid came across the room and closed the shutters. Lisa turned away and surveyed her uncluttered room. A large bed with its woven coverlet, a capacious wardrobe and chest of drawers. Lisa gazed in dismay at the old-fashioned washstand.

In halting Spanish she asked about the bath. The maid smilingly indicated a room across the corridor. It was indeed a bathroom but again a dismayed Lisa realised there were no bath taps. The water, the maid informed her, would be heated and brought up to her.

Lisa returned to her room, surrounded by the suitcases she had no heart to unpack. The day had started out so well, with such joyful anticipation. How different was her arrival to have been. She still could not cry for her father; he had been little more than a stranger for years but her heart ached for her loss just the same.

Beyond the shutters she could hear the endless, and hitherto unfamiliar, chatter of the crickets and chicadas, interrupted from time to time by the throaty gurgle of a bull frog. It was all so frightening. Here she was in a strange and slightly alien land — a country that had taken her father from her — without friends or family. Except for the president who had appointed himself a father-figure and she would be eternally grateful to him for his kindness.

Wearily she lifted one of her suitcases onto the bed and unfastened the locks. Major Meredith's photograph stared up at her from among the folds of her clothes. She was startled at the sudden confrontation with her father and picked up the photograph carefully, studying it, searching it for some explanation.

'I shall never know you now,' she whispered before placing it prominently on the chest of drawers.

It was as she unpacked the rest of her clothes that she remembered putting the photograph at the bottom of the case when she had packed hastily on board the tanker earlier in the day.

She frowned in concentration; she was sure she had put it underneath her clothes not on top. She turned out the rest of the contents until she found the companion photograph — the one of her mother — and she placed it thoughtfully on the chest. She *had* put them together she was sure. But it didn't make sense.

There was a sharp knock at the door. '*Agua caliente señorita!*'

The puzzle was put firmly out of her mind by the arrival of her bathwater. She would resolve it another time.

2

When she was shown into a small salon later that evening Lisa found the president waiting for her, a glass of sherry in his hand. At the sight of him she was glad she had changed into an ordinary cotton dress; the president wore another suit but it was equally as shabby as its predecessor.

'A sherry my dear? I have it shipped direct from Jerez.'

Lisa came into the room and accepted a glass of sherry from an ancient negro butler wearing an old-fashioned wing collar.

'I hope you feel refreshed after your rest,' he enquired.

'Yes, it was quite a luxury having a bath instead of a shower like I had to have on board the tanker.'

'And your room is satisfactory?'

'Very much so.'

'You must feel free to ask for anything you require. My staff are at your disposal.' Lisa smiled her appreciation. The president swung around and for the first time she saw they were not alone in the room. A high-backed chair was occupied by a woman whose black hair and dark brown eyes proclaimed her Spanish heritage. So pale was her skin in contrast it could have been carved out of alabaster. The dress she wore was of excellent cut but several years out of fashion as indicated by its length. Her dainty feet hardly touched the floor and were it not for her hair, severely piled on top of her head, Lisa could have been forgiven for mistaking her for a child. On closer scrutiny she realised she was only a year or two younger than herself.

'Allow me to introduce my daughter Inés,' President Pantero said with obvious pride.

Lisa knew she had been at a disadvantage; the girl had had plenty of time to assess her unseen. Lisa smiled and extended her hand. 'I'm delighted to meet you Señorita Pantero.'

Inés Pantero smiled too but the expression in her eyes was as unfathomable as Captain Baldera's had been. 'I am pleased to meet you too Lisa, but I am also sorry your arrival had to be such a sad one.'

Inés grasped Lisa's hand briefly and it's touch was cool and smooth. Lisa immediately liked the president's daughter, feeling, guiltily, her cool ineffusive welcome far more acceptable than that of her father.

During the meal Lisa could bring herself to do no more than pick at the strange food placed in front of her, although her senses told her it was delicious. Her head ached abominably and there was a stronger pain in her heart. She really didn't want to stay in Santa Angelina but there was little in England she was eager to return to. If only she hadn't set her heart on living here . . .

'You do not like our food?' President Pantero asked.

Before Lisa could reply Inés broke in. 'Really Papa you are so thoughtless. Lisa has had a long and tiring journey ending in tragedy. I should have been very much surprised if she had eaten heartily.'

Lisa smiled her thanks across the table. Behind their inscrutible faces Spaniards seemed to be as feeling as anyone, she thought.

'Of course,' the president agreed, 'it *was* very thoughtless. You must rest as much as possible during the next few days. Our climate is quite temperate but newcomers always take a while to adjust.'

Once more in the salon Inés poured coffee. 'Your dress is very pretty,' she remarked as she handed Lisa the cup. 'Is that how short the skirts are being worn now?'

'Some are worn much shorter than this,' Lisa replied with a laugh, 'but I think this is as far as I should go.'

Inés laughed too. 'I will have to shorten my skirts too. It is very difficult to be fashionable in Santa Angelina. My last wardrobe was bought on my way back from school in Europe. Fortunately most other women on the island are in the same position.'

Lisa leaned forward. 'I have some recent magazines in my room if you would like to borrow them.'

Inés Pantero's face lit up with an unexpected smile. 'That is most kind of you.'

Lisa sat back in her chair, happy and confident that she had acquired a friend of her own age. She glanced at her host and wondered if his invitation had something to do with a desire to provide a companion for his daughter.

'Your Excellency . . . ' she began.

The president held up one hand in protest. 'Please,' he said, 'I am a man of the people.' He touched his chest. 'Just an ordinary man.'

'Señor Pantero,' she began again, 'is it possible for me to visit my father's grave tomorrow?'

'My dear,' he said softly, 'I hesitate to deepen your sorrow but as I have already told you Major Meredith died in the hills and it was several days before the survivors returned.' He paused. 'Here in the tropics it would not be wise to bring back the bodies.'

Lisa blinked back a tear and biting her lip she replied, 'I didn't realise.'

President Pantero's face was hard when he spoke again. 'You can be assured Lisa, the culprits will be brought to justice.'

'It won't bring him back,' she said with an involuntary shudder.

'No but it will prevent a similar tragedy in the future and I am sure you would want that.'

Lisa looked at him appealingly. 'What kind of people are these?'

He shook his head sadly. 'That, I am ashamed to say, I cannot tell you. These revolutionaries have been a thorn in my flesh for several years now and there seems to be a conspiracy of silence surrounding them.

'They operate from the hills and so far they have not strayed into the plains, but I believe they are becoming more bold.' His lips curled derisively. 'There is a leader they call El Salvador — the saviour. As to his real identity and the identity of his followers I do not know.' He shrugged expressively. 'But I will find out. There are supporters of these murderers all over the island but Captain Baldera is efficient too, and loyal. I surround myself with only the most loyal people.'

Lisa's head reeled. It was all too fantastic to be true. Yet to her sorrow she knew it must be.

'There I have upset you once again. It will be better if you go to your room. We have tired you with all this talk.'

Lisa shook her head. 'Not yet. I want to know. I must know what my father died for. Please tell me — tell me what these people want.'

'Quite simple my dear — power. El Salvador wants to become the president of Santa Angelina. He is an ambitious man.' He leaned forward eagerly. 'We are a poor people Lisa. There is much poverty and disease on this island and because of these men I have to channel most of our income into our defence budget instead of improving our lot. In this way I am playing into their hands — I, the man voted into office by the majority of the people. And I have served my people well for more than thirty years.'

Lisa got slowly to her feet. 'I *am* tired. Will you excuse me for this evening Señor Pantero?'

He stood up too. 'Of course, my dear. Sleep well.'

She went towards the door and paused. 'And thank you for explaining. I feel better knowing what my father was helping to do — or prevent.' She turned to Inés. 'I will bring those magazines before I go to bed.'

'No, no. Please do not trouble tonight,' she protested. 'Tomorrow will do.'

'It's no trouble and you may as well have them to look through.'

By the time she reached her room her mind was fogged with fatigue and all the information she had been given during the evening. She reached for her last unopened suitcase and put it on the bed. The magazines lay on the top and as she lifted them out she caught sight of her writing case underneath them. She put the magazines on the bed and lifted the case.

It had been a present from her father on her sixteenth birthday; so she would have no excuse not to write to him, he had said. Through the years they had kept up a regular correspondence but mainly about the island and never about his work.

Her hands shook slightly as she unzipped it. Perhaps there was something in them she had missed. Something that would point a finger to show her how he had felt about the struggle within the island.

Lisa stared in dismay at the blank

writing paper that fluttered onto the coverlet. She searched them frenziedly but her father's letters had gone.

At first she was bewildered and then bewilderment turned to anger. Some-one had taken them; it was the only explanation. The letters had certainly been there first thing this morning. She remembered checking the last one for the arrangements.

All she had left of her father — and now they were gone!

For a few minutes she could do nothing more than stare helplessly down at the blank paper and then she turned and ran blindly out of the room and back down the corridor, heedless of the noise she was making on the tiled floor. She was aware of two startled faces turning as she burst into the salon.

'Someone has taken my father's letters,' she gasped.

The president calmly led her to a chair and pushed her into it. 'Now,' he said, 'tell us what has happened.'

'I kept all the letters my father ever sent me since he came here. When I was getting the magazines for Inés I opened my writing case . . . I felt the need to read them tonight . . . and they were gone.'

'But this is most puzzling. Are you sure you have not mislaid them elsewhere?'

She shook her head. 'I always keep them there and they *were* definitely there this morning.'

President Pantero moved away, inclining his head thoughtfully. 'Why should anyone want your letters?'

'I don't know. They were personal — just ordinary letters in fact.'

'Then it must be a mistake. I will tell Baldera; He will make enquiries. Inés will ask amongst the servants. Unless they have been destroyed they will be found.'

By now the initial shock was wearing off and she felt foolish. She had made a fuss over nothing. What did a few letters from a dead man matter? Only to herself.

She rose for the second time. 'I'm sorry to cause you this trouble. Please don't bother. It doesn't really matter.'

'Nonsense. It matters a great deal. We will find out. And now Inés, escort our guest back to her room. She is in great need of a rest.'

★ ★ ★

Throughout the ensuing days Lisa didn't venture out of the grounds of the house; she had no wish to. She saw little of her host even at meal times and little more of Inés. The arrangement suited Lisa; she needed time to analyse her own feelings. At the moment she was in a void; yesterday was dead and she was afraid to face tomorrow.

The headache that had developed on the first day still hovered around her and she was unable to dispel the general feeling of unease. Inés put it down to the climate or the water, or grief. Lisa agreed it was probably a little of each, although she could hardly explain she hadn't known her father well enough to grieve for him to such an extent and she was continually called upon to refuse Inés's well-intentioned offer to send for a doctor. Lisa knew the malaise that afflicted her was not physical.

The letters failed to appear, which was no more than she expected. She racked her brains to try and find a reason why they had been taken from her case, but there seemed to be no answer.

One morning when she awoke early she lay in her bed aware that there was something different about the day. She lay quite motionless for a few moments before realising a harsh hissing sound was coming from behind the heavy shutters. Lisa leaped out of bed and flung them back. She laughed in amazement to see the almost solid sheet of water blinding her view of the garden below. She had been warned of tropical rainstorms but could never have imagined them to be this violent.

An hour later the sun was shining once more in an incredibly blue sky and it was as if the rain had never happened. Lisa's headache had disappeared and for the first time since her arrival she wanted to take an interest in her surroundings.

Both the president and Inés were present at lunch and they both watched with satisfaction as their guest at last did justice to the food that was put before her.

'You are looking much better today,' President Pantero remarked, helping himself to a purple skinned passion fruit.

'I feel it,' she replied, finishing the last morsel of savoury tortilla. 'Perhaps the rain cleared my head as well as the air outside.'

'You will find it very pleasant in the garden this afternoon,' Inés told her and then glanced at her father somewhat hesitantly, 'We shall have to arrange some entertainment for Lisa now she is feeling better.'

'Please don't trouble on my behalf,' she begged.

President Pantero waved a pudgy hand in the air. 'I have been considering holding a reception in your honour so that you can meet all your father's friends.'

Lisa flushed with pleasure. 'That would be lovely. He rarely mentioned his friends in his letters but I'm sure he must have had some.'

'He did indeed. They will all be anxious to meet you. In fact my staff have had several enquiries about you since your arrival.' He turned to smile at his daughter. 'I imagine they think we have locked Lisa up in el alcazar and are keeping her there by force.'

Inés did not seem to find this amusing but Lisa laughed. 'Why on earth should they think you'd do that?'

'It was only a joke,' Inés replied, hurriedly, looking down at her plate.

Her father continued to beam, sitting back comfortably in his chair. 'Since the outbreak of terrorist activities on the island I have had to be most careful. I take every precaution, you understand. And it has become something of a joke. They might just think I am keeping you under lock and key for your own safety. Not that there is any need for you to be alarmed; when the rebels come into the town they are disguised as ordinary people. There has never been any trouble in the towns and villages. They would not dare. It was only my stupid joke.'

'I'm not at all alarmed Señor Pantero,' Lisa replied, cutting into the skin of an orange that had been growing on a tree that very morning. 'I have nothing to fear from these men surely; just because I am Major Meredith's daughter. I should think they are more frightened than I am.' Inés and her father both frowned and Lisa decided to drop the subject. But she could not find it in her heart to hate the men who had killed her father. From her knowledge of foreign affairs she knew it was probably poverty and hunger that had driven them to such desperate measures, as it had done in countless other countries. There was no point in saying this to the president who no doubt knew it as well as she, and for him it would be a very touchy and worrying subject.

The president rose from his chair. 'Not for public servants the idle life,' he said with a benign smile. 'I must go now and attend to matters of state. I shall try and squeeze some more money out of the budget.' He glanced at his daughter. 'We shall have to see if we can allow Dr. Rodriguez some modern equipment for his hospital.'

Lisa noticed the quick flush that spread up Inés' usually pale cheeks as she averted her eyes.

Her father continued with a dramatic sigh. 'But owing to the unfortunate military situation I may have to order some heavier artillery instead. It is a shame but we must safeguard our security.' His face brightened. 'But I must not depress our guest with our troubles. No doubt the terrorist problem will be solved in time. At least I have some good news for *you* Lisa . . . '

Lisa looked at him expectantly and he continued. 'Your letters have been found.'

'Where?' she asked eagerly.

'One of the maids discovered them as she was about to burn some rubbish. You are most fortunate she was observant. They could very easily have gone up in smoke.' He beamed benevolently. 'It was all a careless mistake. No doubt they were taken in error along with the rubbish.'

Lisa opened her mouth to protest. It was impossible for them to have been taken by mistake from a zipped case that had been lying in a suitcase. But at the sight of the president's satisfied face she replied, 'As long as I have them back it doesn't really matter. May I know the maid who found them? I should like to thank her personally.'

'It is better you do not,' Inés replied

softly. 'They have been reprimanded for their carelessness so it is hardly in order to thank one of them.' She pushed her chair back. 'Excuse me; I must start to make arrangements and prepare a guest list for the reception.'

The president followed her to the door. 'And if you will come to my office, Lisa, I shall let you have the letters.'

★ ★ ★

Lisa found her favourite seat beneath the shade of a towering eucalyptus tree. During her stay at the aptly named 'La Casa des flores' she had spent a great deal of time in the garden that had given the house its name. She never tired of the endless variety of weird and wonderful plants and trees it contained. She loved the multi-hued hibiscus that seemed to spill its colour everywhere and she marvelled at the bougainvillea that transformed an ordinary wall into a living mass of purple and red. Everywhere palm trees sprouted, from the majestic royal palm towering proudly above all others to its brother, the lowly cabbage palm, with its less attractive rubbery leaves.

She sat for a long while just holding the letters in her hand, watching the antics of an emerald-breasted humming bird that was fluttering from tree to tree, its long tail feathers perked cheekily, quite undisturbed by her presence nearby.

There was hardly a sound to be heard except for the singing of the ever present breeze through the leaves. It was hard for Lisa, amid such peace and beauty, to believe there was discord on the island. She couldn't doubt her letters had been deliberately taken and she shuddered at the thought of a pair of unknown hands searching through her belongings. The dress she wore felt clammy against her skin when she realised the searcher must have handled it too.

She recalled President Pantero telling her that the rebels have supporters everywhere and it occurred to her that there could be a sympathiser actually amongst his own staff, despite his assurance that he surrounds himself with only the most loyal servants. She realised at once she had no idea how widespread was support for the rebel movement and she resolved to find out.

She quickly scanned through the letters, although she already knew them by heart, but when she had finished she was as puzzled as ever. There was simply nothing there to warrant them being stolen and no doubt that was why they had been returned.

Her attention was drawn from the mystery of where the letters had been for more than a week by heavy footsteps coming in her direction. The path was obscured by a row of jacarandas and she gave a start of surprise when she saw Captain Baldera turn the corner.

He seemed equally surprised to see

her and after hesitating for a moment he bowed stiffly and said, 'Señorita Meredith I am pleased to see you are now well.'

Despite the fact that he was only a year or two older than herself Lisa found the captain rather a daunting person. Perhaps it was because when he smiled it was with his lips and not with his eyes; and his eyes never revealed his feelings for a second.

Remembering his abrupt way with her on the first day Lisa found she couldn't respond too pleasantly to his perfunctory remark. 'I wasn't ill Captain Baldera. But thank you for your concern.'

His eyes travelled to the letters she was still clutching in her hands. 'I see your letters have been returned to you intact. The maids have been reprimanded for their carelessness. It is a most regrettable error.'

It suddenly occurred to Lisa that rather more importance was being attached to the letters than she herself had done and it was beginning to intrigue her. But aloud she said, 'It is of no importance Captain. I should hate anyone to get into trouble on my account. I hope His Excellency hasn't wasted his time in finding them for me when affairs of state are so pressing.'

'We were only too pleased to be of service to you Señorita Meredith, especially as the loss was entirely due to our stupidity. It would be unfortunate indeed if you were to get entirely the wrong impression of Santa Angelina on your first day here.' He paused for a moment, studying her carefully and then said, 'I wonder, Señorita, if you would allow me to speak to you for a few moments.'

Lisa was momentarily startled and then moved along the iron seat. Captain Baldera sat stiffly by her side and she looked at him expectantly. 'I wish to apologise,' he said at last, with difficulty. Her eyes narrowed fractionally but she said nothing and he went on, 'When I met you last week you no doubt considered me to be a rude man, did you not?'

Lisa shrugged. 'You were doing your duty. I don't suppose circumstances called upon you to do more.'

'Yes exactly,' he said eagerly. 'But I must explain. His Excellency gave precise orders for you not to be alarmed about Major Meredith's absence. He wanted to be the one to tell you and I was afraid you would ask awkward questions . . . '

Lisa smiled. She guessed Luis Baldera would have difficulty in revealing his feelings in his own language let alone in a foreign one. Despite his stiff manner and grand uniform she suspected he was rather shy when it came to conversing with women. 'I understand perfectly Captain Baldera. You were only trying to spare my feelings.'

Luis Baldera smiled and suddenly Lisa felt years older; he looked such a boy just then.

'I am relieved. Now we can be friends.'

Lisa gave a surprised laugh. 'Of course we will be friends.'

She took his proferred hand and they shook solemnly like a pair of children. His face became solemn once more. 'I knew your father and he was a brave man. We will miss him.'

For Lisa what promised to be an interesting exchange was interrupted by the sound of voices coming from the house itself. Lisa stared towards the veranda in time to see Inés coming down the steps towards them. She was not alone. Accompanying her was a tall, slim man whom Lisa had never seen before. His curly hair and magnificent, almost black, eyes were as dark as Inés', but his skin was the light olive of most Spaniards. From the lightweight suit he wore she presumed he was not like Luis Baldera in the army although his straight carriage indicated he might well be. Inés, dwarfed by his height, wore a more animated expression of her face than Lisa had seen up until now. As they approached, unaware of being observed, Lisa glanced at Luis Baldera and he too was watching the other couple and the inscrutible expression had returned to his face.

When they were a few yards away Inés and her companion saw them and their conversation abruptly ceased. The smile on Inés face disappeared and her expression hardened for a second before the smile returned. The man simply stared at Lisa without attempting to veil his curiosity.

Lisa found herself colouring under his critical gaze which travelled downwards and lingered on her bare legs and expanse of thigh revealed by her short skirt. She wondered if he was a man who didn't know fashion governed the length of a woman's skirt. She had heard how puritanical the Spanish could be and it was obvious even the wealthier inhabitants of Santa Angelina were several years behind the times in that respect.

Inés and her companion came forward; now Inés was smiling broadly.

Captain Baldera jumped hastily to his feet in her presence.

'Good afternoon Captain. I see you are enjoying the sun.'

Lisa hid her smile at Inés' superior manner. She wondered if she was always so condescendingly regal with her father's staff.

'I was on my way to see His Excellency. Please excuse me.' He nodded to the newcomer and strode manfully towards the house.

Lisa stole another glance at the man to find he was still staring at her quite fiercely, and she could not hold his gaze. Inés stared after Captain Baldera for a moment or two and then turned back to her companion.

'It is an opportune moment for you to meet Miss Meredith Miguel. Lisa this is our dear friend Dr. Miguel Rodriguez.'

So this was the man the mere mention of whom made Inés flush. Lisa was now consumed with curiosity as to their relationship, although it was fairly obvious it was a close one.

Miguel Rodriguez took her hand gravely and from the disturbing way his eyes never left her face she gained the distinct impression he was seeking the answer to some question. 'I was acquainted with your father, Miss Meredith,' he said. 'He will be missed by his friends.'

Lisa reluctantly met his eyes once more as she took his hand and at the same time she almost recoiled from the impact of the contempt she saw in them. Before she could bring herself to reply he had turned back to Inés, with the effect of having said his piece and he was now dismissing her. Lisa was shocked once again to see the harsh lines of his face soften as he smiled at her and said 'I must go Inés. I will see you again soon.' He turned back to Lisa and said more formally 'Goodbye Miss Meredith.'

'Goodbye Dr. Rodriguez,' she replied, more calmly than she felt, as he turned and quickly walked back to the house.

Lisa watched him go, a frown

creasing her brow, wondering if the length of her skirt could have prompted the active dislike she had plainly seen.

'What was Captain Baldera talking to you about?' Inés demanded, sitting down in the place he had vacated.

It was irritating for Lisa to have to explain a personal conversation but in deference to her hostess she said, 'Captain Baldera was simply giving his condolences. He explained why he couldn't the day I arrived.' She paused for a moment and then said, 'I hope Dr. Rodriguez's presence doesn't mean someone is ill.'

A smile curved Inés lips. 'No, no-one is ill. Miguel comes to see me.'

3

Lisa moved along the tables steeply banked with a dazzling array of delicious food. To give Inés her due she had arranged things splendidly. Enough food had been provided to feed the entire population of Santa Angelina. Almost everything, from the whole roast sucking pigs — *lechon asado* — turkeys, baked crabs and lobsters to the baskets of exotic passion fruit, ortaniques, guavas, mangoes and bananas had been reared or grown within the island.

Inés, looking startlingly beautiful in a blood red dress with a full length flounced skirt in traditional Spanish style, sparkled like the champagne that was being served. She darted like a vivacious butterfly, obviously enjoying every moment. Half hidden in one corner a trio played sambas and rhumbas discreetly beneath the babble of voices conversing in lisping Spanish, punctuated occasionally by drawling English.

The vast hall downstairs thronged with people, some of whom had already been introduced to Lisa. The object of holding the reception had been for her to meet her father's friends but she doubted that her father had known all these people; he was never this sociable and in view of the chronic poverty suffered by the people of Santa Angelina she was far from happy at having such a lavish reception held in her name.

She wandered around the hall smiling at the guests — few of whom she could converse with as most of them could speak Spanish only — and sipping at her drink in an attempt to make it last as long as possible. There were a great many Generals and Colonels of the Santa Angelinan army in the gathering — to Lisa there seemed more than was really necessary for a small republic.

Her arm was suddenly caught in a claw-like hand tipped with scarlet nail varnish. 'Enjoying yourself Miss Meredith?' asked Mrs. Byer, the American Consul's wife. She was a plump woman with blonde hair and a fleshy wrinkled face.

'Very much Mrs. Byer. Would you like another drink?'

'My wife has had enough,' her husband, a tired-looking little man, replied.

'Nonsense,' his wife argued, staring defiantly at him. 'I shall certainly have another when the tray comes round.'

She turned her watery eyes on Lisa again. 'And how long do you aim to be staying on this God-forgotten island?'

'I haven't decided. His Excellency has been kind enough to invite me to stay indefinitely.'

The woman laid her hand on Lisa's arm again. 'I can't imagine why anyone should stay here *voluntarily*.' She flashed an angry glance at her husband whose nose was deep in his glass. 'Your poor dear father could pick and choose where he worked. There must be a dozen other countries needing trained and experienced soldiers and yet he stayed here.' She smiled sympathetically at Lisa. 'Not that it matters now of course. Sad, so sad.

'When I married Henry I believed he would either stay in the diplomatic corps in the States or at least in London or Paris. Somewhere *civilised*. Do you know our electricity is run from a generator *and* it's always breaking down. The servants are idle too. Can't get them to clean properly. And did you notice the smell around the harbour? We'll die of some horrible disease I'm sure. And now we're not even safe in our beds. Who knows when these revolutionaries will strike at us. We Americans always bear the brunt when there's a civil war.'

Her husband transferred his bored attention from his drink for the moment. 'Now, now Hatty. It's not that bad.'

'Bad enough,' she countered and then

turned back to Lisa who was listening with scarcely concealed amusement. She made no attempt to reply to her grievances and knew that none was required; Mrs. Byer was happy enough to have a new pair of ears to listen to her complaints. 'What do you think of El Presidente, Miss Meredith? A charming man isn't he?'

Lisa wasn't sure whether Mrs. Byer was being sarcastic or not, but replied levelly, 'Señor Pantero has been kindness itself since my arrival.'

Mrs. Byer sniffed. 'He's all right I guess — as long as you're on the right side of him. I've heard some pretty hair raising stories of goings on in that fortress.' She tossed her blonde head in the general direction of el alcazar.

'There are always exaggerated stories about these places Mrs. Byer. I'm sure as a prison it's no better or worse than any other.'

She sniffed again and then her lips curled into a derisive smile as she gazed over Lisa's shoulder. 'Well now look who's here.'

Lisa turned in time to see Miguel Rodriguez being greeted by the president himself. Inés too hurried forward and they were swallowed up momentarily by the crowd, but not before Lisa noticed how striking his dark looks were against the white of his dinner jacket. On their previous encounter she had been too disturbed by his alien attitude to notice his appearance. She did not have time to consider why his brusque manner towards her had troubled her many times since their encounter in the garden, for Mrs. Byer started to speak again.

She winked knowingly. 'If you ask me that is one young man who knows exactly where he's going.'

'Do you mean Dr. Rodriguez?' Lisa asked ingenuously.

'Who else?' the woman retorted, helping herself to another glass of champagne from the proffered tray. 'Although he hardly merits the title.'

She gave an expressive shudder. 'I'd rather die than have him touch me again.' She lowered her voice a fraction. 'We always go back to civilisation for any medical treatment but two years ago I nearly died; appendicitis and there was simply no alternative but to go into that museum of a hospital. It was a miracle I lived I tell you.'

Her husband stirred and muttered. 'It was all quite straight-forward.'

Hatty Byer turned her back pointedly to her husband. 'That's what he said, to cover up his own incompetence but I was the one in agony. The sisters were no better. Never spoke a word and from their faces you'd think they couldn't hear either. Do you know I had to share a ward with two dozen *peasants*?'

'How shocking,' Lisa commiserated, trying with little success to keep her face straight, but the garrulous woman was too carried away to notice.

'Can you imagine that?' She raised her eyes to the ceiling. 'There was a time I just prayed I would die. I just could not get through to that man. He ignored all my complaints. I told Henry if anything should happen to me he should be charged with gross negligence. The day after the operation — and I dare not *think* what the operating theatre is like — he told the sisters to put screens round my bed. It wasn't much but at least if I couldn't have a private suite it was something — until I heard that wicked man say it was to keep me from disturbing the other patients. Patients! I tell you most of them had never slept in a bed before!

'After that I thanked providence that from that day onwards I saw only Dr. Lim. Have you met him yet?'

Lisa managed to shake her head before Mrs. Byer continued. 'He's a very nice man. A Chinese of course and only a physician but so sympathetic. Back in the States the surgeon visits his patient twice a day until she's discharged. But of course you can't expect that kind of civility here . . . '

Lisa glanced around in the hope that

someone would come and rescue her. It might have been amusing to have seen how Miguel Rodriguez handled the whining Mrs. Byer and she was sure he was just the man to do it. Although her one brief meeting had given her no cause to admire him, his dealing with the American lady certainly did.

'Which makes me wonder what a man like that is doing here,' Mrs. Byer continued thoughtfully.

'Doing his job just like anyone else,' Lisa said absently, realising no help was at present coming.

'I wonder, I really do. He was born here you know — a descendant of one of the orginal Conquistadores like all the other Spaniards around here. They're all so proud of it too, even though they were all butchers.' She shot a malicious glance at Miguel Rodriguez who at that moment, accompanied by Inés, was talking to a group of people at the other side of the hall. 'I shouldn't be surprised if *that* one is descended from one of the Spanish Inquisition. He was brought up and educated in the States and that was what fooled me at first. Our nice Dr. Masters back home has a beautiful home with servants to wait on him and he drives a Lincoln Continental. Why should a man like Miguel Rodriguez give up the chance of all that to come here? I heard he worked in the Wilton Clinic for a while. After that I imagine he could write out his own pay cheque. It seems very fishy to me. Perhaps he did something dreadful and had to leave the States. After all they don't ask questions in these parts. We may be surrounded by Nazi war criminals for all we know. Now if he'd been *German* I wouldn't have let him come within a mile of me.'

Lisa was fast getting annoyed with the silly woman and said rather sharply, 'Not everyone wants expensive houses or cars Mrs. Byer. Whatever his reasons for coming here you should be glad of getting such expert help when you needed it.'

Mrs. Byer looked as though she was

about to reply to that when she caught sight of Inés and said softly, 'If he has any affection left over from that hospital full of dead-beats we all know who it's for. Perhaps he's aiming to be the next El Presidente. That could be the answer don't you think?'

Lisa was weak with relief at the sight of Inés coming directly towards them. Her face wore the most regal of smiles. 'I do hope you are enjoying yourselves,' she said.

Mrs. Byer smiled broadly. 'It's a wonderful party my dear, as always. I always do say His Excellency never spares expense or trouble when entertaining his friends. And you my dear, how charming you look tonight. I'll just bet every young man in the room is torn between looking at you and Miss Meredith, although in your case I'm sure it's just one man.'

Lisa felt stifled by the woman's blatent hypocrisy but Inés said quite calmly, 'Thank you Mrs. Byer. May I take Lisa for a moment? We have some people over here who are very anxious to meet her.'

Lisa did not hesitate. She began to move away but the American woman was not finished. Her pink face crumpled. 'That's very mean of you Inés. Miss Meredith and I were just having a very nice conversation.'

'We'll finish it another time.' Lisa replied, hurriedly following Inés.

Inés looked at her impishly the moment they were out of earshot. 'I saw you wilting a long time ago but I thought it best to let her get everything out of her system and then she will leave you alone.'

Lisa laughed. 'Is she always like this?'

'Oh yes, always. But she is the American Consul's wife and must be treated with respect. Apart from that she is a surprisingly good source of information; gossips always are. They never guard their tongues.'

Lisa followed Inés into a small ante-room set out with small tables.

Several of the tables were already occupied by guests who had tired of the crush and had retired to this quiet corner to eat their food. Inés unhesitatingly led her to one of the tables occupied by a middle-aged couple.

The man, who was about fifty, well-built, his fair hair bleached white by the sun, rose from his chair when he saw them approach.

'I have found her for you,' Inés said to them and then turned to Lisa. 'This is Mr. and Mrs. Philip Bannerman — friends of Major Meredith.'

The name rang a loud bell in Lisa's mind. She had definately heard it mentioned, and before she had come to the island. An old half-buried resentment reared again when she remembered where she had heard it. Three years before her father had opted to spend his leave on the island at a holiday bungalow belonging to people called Bannerman, instead of coming home to spend it with her.

Philip Bannerman shook her hand

heartily. 'We've been longing to meet you Lisa. Won't you sit down and join us?'

Lisa thankfully sat down as Inés excused herself to return to the guests. 'This is my wife Mary,' the man added.

Mary Bannerman looked more like Philip's sister than his wife so marked was their likeness. 'We enquired about you last week,' she said, 'I hope you weren't too ill.'

Lisa laughed. 'Not really. I think it was a case of being literally under the weather.'

'The climate often affects people like that,' Philip remarked, 'and of course you had a dreadful shock to face too.'

The ineffusive friendliness of the Bannermans was refreshing to Lisa after her enervating conversation with Mrs. Byer and she could not help but warm to them, especially as they were so definitely English.

'If there is anything we can do . . . ' Mrs. Bannerman said hesitantly.

'Thank you. Everyone has been very kind.'

'Would you like a drink?' Philip broke in hastily.

Lisa shook her head. 'I've had quite enough.'

'You must visit us,' his wife added, 'we'll introduce you to a real rum punch.'

Lisa laughed. 'That sounds very nice.' She paused for a second and then asked, 'You were close friends of my father?'

'We like to think so Lisa,' Philip said.

'I remember,' she said with some difficulty, 'he wrote to say he spent his leave with you three years ago.'

Philip Bannerman exchanged glances with his wife. 'Er . . . yes, he did. We have a small bungalow at the other side of the island, near a small fishing village. No more than a few huts really but the beach is really beautiful. We go there as often as we can manage with Rowena — she's our daughter.' He paused. 'Your father was very tired Lisa

71

and that was why he didn't go back home. He needed that rest very badly. He worked very hard — much harder than really was necessary. But I expect you already know that.'

Lisa looked down at her hands clasped tightly in the lap of her green silk evening gown and wanted to cry out 'No I didn't! I didn't know anything about him!' And that hurt more than his death. She raised her head to meet Philip's eyes, 'And all these people? Were they his friends too?'

Philip Bannerman sat back in his chair and laced his hands on the table. 'Most of them were acquaintances I should think. On a small island such as this there is a very closely knit social structure — everyone knows everyone else. It's like a small village or suburb.'

'A reception like this,' his wife added, 'especially when a newcomer is on view, is a real event. There's very little else in the way of a social life.'

Lisa relaxed in their company, finding she was liking these people more and more and her prejudice against them was melting rapidly. 'Are you with the army Mr. Bannerman?'

'Philip. No, civilian. We have a small sugar plantation twelve kilometres from here. It's not the most lucrative of businesses these days but after thirty years on the island it's become a way of life.' He took hold of his wife's hand. 'I brought Mary back from London after one visit twenty years ago.'

'When we were in London five years ago we couldn't wait to get back,' his wife said. 'It was all so dirty and noisy. And to think I used to work there!'

'Yes,' Philip added, 'I'm afraid we've become natives.'

More guests had filtered into the room. The trio were bringing in their instruments. 'It looks as though there's going to be some dancing,' Mary said. 'Inés usually gets her own way, although her father doesn't exactly approve. Dancing isn't considered dignified.'

The band began to play but the floor

remained empty. Lisa turned to Philip. 'Why isn't anyone dancing?'

His eyes danced with amusement. 'Protocol says we must wait for the president.'

A sudden hush descended on the gathering as President Pantero, his arm linked with his daughter's, appeared in the doorway. Lisa thought he looked just like a comic opera character in his elaborate uniform emblazoned with medals and ribbons, but no-one else seemed to find him amusing. He handed his daughter to a young man standing nearby and the music started up again. Soon the floor was filled with whirling couples and to Lisa the whole scene had a slightly unreal quality.

Was it only a fortnight ago that she was feverishly packing her belongings in the cold of a London spring? A few thousand miles, but a whole world away from this little island that somehow had been left behind the rest.

A shadow appeared at her side, breaking into her thoughts and she looked up sharply. She had forgotten Luis Baldera after speaking to him briefly earlier in the evening. He too looked very striking in full dress uniform, but Lisa was slightly repulsed by the pistol he always wore quite prominently.

He exchanged a few polite words with the Bannermans and Lisa guessed there was no real warmth on either side. Then he turned to Lisa and said stiffly and precisely, 'I should be honoured if you would have this dance with me.'

Lisa followed him to where the other people were dancing. They were mostly the younger people, the older ones having stayed in the hall.

'You are enjoying yourself?' Luis asked as he held her stiffly and propelled her around the room.

'Very much. And you?'

'I am not here to enjoy myself. I am here in charge of the president's safety.'

'Ah. That must be why you always wear a gun.'

'It is a necessity.'

'But surely it isn't necessary tonight — here in his house among friends.'

'It is necessary all the time, Lisa. Not everyone is a friend.'

Lisa flushed uncomfortably at the use of her first name and at his hint that rebel sympathisers might be present. They continued to dance in silence and suddenly she caught sight of Miguel Rodriguez who was standing next to the president. They were both watching her as she danced past. The president beamed and she smiled back hesitantly. Dr. Rodriguez did not smile and Lisa was uncomfortably aware of his dark eyes glittering with an expression she could not read, but she felt frustration rise inside her knowing he was antagonistic towards her but not why.

The music stopped and Luis dropped his hands to his side. 'You will have the next dance?'

Lisa had no real desire to dance with him again; it was too exhausting but she agreed as the music started up again.

'Señorita Pantero is arranging a beach barbecue for next week. You will come with me?'

'Well . . . Luis that would be very nice . . . ' she paused, not really knowing how to reply and he said unexpectedly, 'I should like to get to know you better Lisa.'

Despite his formal way of speaking she was left in little doubt as to what he meant and she wasn't sure she wanted to become more friendly with him; it might create unforeseen complications.

'I'd like to go to the barbecue,' she said at last, feeling this was the safest thing to say.

The music paused for a minute and Lisa was whisked away by another man. Dance followed dance and she was never without a partner. She laughed a great deal and never refused an invitation to dance, but somehow it was only superfluous gaiety; although it was a gay and glittering occasion a strange atmosphere of unease lay beneath the

77

surface and transmitted itself to her.

Some of her partners spoke very little English and even their attempts to converse with her convulsed her with laughter. That problem did not arise with Rafael Jeron whom she learned was a lawyer. He spoke perfect English and was able to tell her amusing stories non-stop the entire time they danced together.

When the music stopped she was reluctant to let him return to his wife; she was learning more about life on the island from his witty anecdotes than she had since her arrival. She sensed someone behind her and turned, laughing, expecting to be whirled onto the floor by yet another young man eager to sample her company, but instead she found herself face to face with Miguel Rodriguez and the smile faded rapidly.

'Miguel!' Rafael greeted him heartily. 'You have come to steal my girl away.'

Miguel smiled. 'You already have one beauty of your own Rafael. You should be ashamed of monopolising another.'

Rafael laughed good-naturedly and went off to find his wife. Without another word Miguel led Lisa onto the floor and she went into his arms easily. He danced well. Her feet had been trodden on many times during the course of the evening but not on this occasion. Despite this she was not relaxed; she danced rigidly in his arms. The bubble had burst; she no longer felt gay and sophisticated but awkward and very young.

She was grateful for being taller than Inés; she could stare over his shoulder instead of at an expanse of white dinner jacket.

'Are you enjoying being the guest of honour?' he asked after a while.

Lisa could not take his question at face value; she was sure it was a barbed one. 'It was very good of the president to hold this reception for me,' she said, very much on her dignity, 'but if I were not here I'm sure he would have held it anyway.'

His lips twitched in amusement. 'You are quite correct Miss Meredith.'

She stared at him angrily. 'You don't approve of me do you Dr. Rodriguez?'

'Approve?' he asked in astonishment. 'Miss Meredith, is it for me to approve or disapprove of you?'

'You know perfectly well what I mean.'

Inés and Luis danced past at that moment, Inés waving gaily. Lisa managed a wan smile. 'Do not trouble yourself about my attitude Miss Meredith,' he said, 'You do not lack suitors and I am too busy to dance attendance too.'

Lisa almost stumbled with vexation. But at least she knew why he disliked her; he obviously considered her to be an empty-headed flirt, come to Santa Angelina for a good time. It was unfair of him to grudge her the first little bit of enjoyment she'd had since she arrived. She recovered quickly and with a coy smile replied, 'But that is exactly what you are doing.'

If she expected him to rise to that she

was disappointed; she was completely disarmed by his answering smile.

To her further disappointment the music stopped just then and gave no sign of starting up again. Miguel kept hold of her arm and led her back to the Bannerman's table. From the sight of their faces it was obvious he was on excellent terms with them, unlike Luis, and Lisa was unaccountably annoyed.

'Do join us Miguel,' Mary said in her quiet way as he held Lisa's chair for her.

'Not just at the moment.' His eyes passed over her and she was left in no doubt it was her presence that prevented him. Tears of humiliation pricked her eyelids and she lowered them for fear someone should see and she kept them downcast until he had gone. She was unwilling to admit to herself that she would have far preferred his attentions to Luis'.

'Why doesn't he like me?' she asked Philip.

He exchanged a meaningful glance

with his wife who said hurriedly, 'It's just his way Lisa. He is terribly overworked and considers these functions a waste of time — only he had to come to please the president.'

Lisa smiled and shrugged philosophically. 'It was rather childish of me to expect to be liked by everyone. I just prefer to know the reason why they don't.'

'We'd like you to come out and visit us one day next week,' Philip said, in an obvious attempt to change the subject and Lisa wondered why.

'I'd like to come — very much,' she replied.

'Monday afternoon?' suggested Mary.

'I shall look forward to that. Tuesday is market day isn't it?' she asked. 'Señor Pantero said it would be interesting for me to see.'

'It's . . . quaint,' Mary agreed and Lisa detected a hint of strain in her voice, especially as she looked anxiously towards her husband.

Lisa, puzzled, said hurriedly, 'Is there

a bus I can catch to your plantation?'

Both Mary and Philip burst out laughing and on seeing Lisa's perplexed frown Philip explained, 'There is a bus that passes quite close to our property but it would be better if I collect you in the station wagon. You wouldn't like to share a twelve kilometre journey with a load of peasants who have never seen soap and rarely water, and all their assorted goats, pigs and chickens.'

'I see what you mean,' Lisa said ruefully, 'I shall take up your offer of a lift in that case.'

The centre of the empty dance floor was taken by a young couple in traditional dress. Everyone's attention was taken by the couple. The man began to strum at his guitar and the girl began to sing a mild mournful song.

'The descendants of the Conquistadores guard their heritage very jealously,' Philip whispered across to her. 'Some families have kept very much to themselves for hundreds of years but most of the early Spanish settlers interbred with

the native women so most of the islanders are a mixture. There are very few
pure-blooded indians left in the Caribbean now.'

They returned their attention to the
couple as the music changed tempo,
becoming louder and more insistent.
The audience's attention switched from
the couple to a dancer who was coming
onto the floor. Lisa started when she
recognised Inés, clicking her heels and
flashing casinets. Her heels began to
thud the floor in time to the beat of the
guitar, interpreting the music with
every move of her body.

The sound and sight was hypnotic;
all eyes were on Inés and so were Lisa's
but her mind kept returning unwillingly
to the enigma of Miguel Rodriguez and
it was more than a case of hurt pride.

There was no sound apart from the
throbbing of the music and Inés's heels
on the tiled floor. It amazed Lisa that
all these people — who were mostly of
Spanish descent — had probably never
even seen the land of their forefathers

yet through four centuries the traditions had remained intact.

Her eyes wandered away from Inés, around the transfixed faces of the audience and they alighted on the solitary figure of Miguel Rodriguez who was standing against the opposite wall, his arms folded and his eyes admiringly on Inés. Suddenly, as if aware of her scrutiny, his eyes met hers and flushing she quickly looked away.

The music stopped as abruptly as it had started, the audience applauding wildly as the trio ran from the room. Suddenly the air was overwhelmingly hot and Lisa slipped quietly out of the room while everyone was still discussing Inés' excellent dancing.

She went through the almost deserted hall, the tables now completely denuded of food, and past the president who was at his charming best, holding court with a group of smartly dressed Americans from the oil refinery.

She shivered in the breeze as she went down the veranda steps. The grounds were full of shadowy figures laughing and whispering in the sweet-scented dusk. Lisa was wandering down the paths in a desultory way when she heard someone walking purposefully towards her. Her heart sank when she turned and recognised Luis approaching.

'I saw you coming onto the veranda,' he said when he came up to her.

'I needed some fresh air.'

'You should have told me *querida*.' It is not good for a pretty young woman to walk around by herself.'

Lisa was glad of the dark that hid her confusion at his use of the endearment and the caressing tone of his voice. He was a good looking young man in an important position; she only wished she could feel attracted to him.

She cleared her throat noisily. 'Where do you live Luis?' she asked lightly, in the hope that he would be side-tracked from his romantic mood.

He smiled and she groaned inwardly, realising her mistake. 'Up at El Alcazar de Maximo Cortes.' He laughed softly. 'But you would never find your way to my quarters. It is better I should come to you.'

'I was merely curious Captain,' she replied in her most quelling way. 'If you dare to attempt to come to my room I will raise the whole household.'

His face hardened and Lisa was shocked to see the latent cruelty there. Involuntarily she backed away and pressed herself against the trunk of a mango tree. He stepped forward and took her chin between his thumb and first finger, forcing her to look at him. 'Tell me *querida* why do you flirt so outrageously with every man you see? Do you not know where it can lead?'

She tried to pull away but she was caught in a vice. 'Let me go,' she said as calmly as she could. But she could only struggle helplessly as he kissed her unwilling lips. He was only able to brush them briefly before an icy voice said in Spanish, 'His Excellency requires your presence Captain.'

He jumped away from Lisa who spun round to see Miguel Rodriguez staring angrily at Luis. For a second or two they faced each other, Luis' face livid with impotent rage, before he turned abruptly and strode back towards the house.

Lisa, feeling slightly sick at the unexpectedly nasty turn of events, made to pass him but he said quite kindly, 'Mary asked me to bring your wrap out to you.' He draped it around her shoulders.

'Thank you,' she murmured, unable to look at him.

'You are not used to our climate. In fact,' he added with a smile, 'you are not used to many things in Santa Angelina and until you are you should not be allowed out on your own.'

She tried to answer but her voice died in her throat so she just allowed him to take her arm and lead her back into the house.

4

The sun was high in a cloudless sky when Lisa sank back in her seat next to Philip Bannerman in his station wagon. The road out of Alhaja de mar descended steeply into a valley.

From the open window Lisa sniffed an unpleasant smell just before she saw a sprawling and decaying shanty town they were passing on the edge of town. Rubbish was rotting between ramshackle huts of rough wood planks with corrugated iron roofs. Slatternly women in rags and naked children turned to stare as the car bumped along the rutted road. Lisa's nose wrinkled with distaste and her eyes stared unbelievingly at the squalor. Matted dogs bayed loudly at them and the children chased skinny fowls that were strutting round the rubbish.

She was relieved when the eyesore

was left behind and all that could be seen were palm spotted fields bordered by white hibiscus hedges on the one hand and the shimmering sea with its margin of silvery sand on the other — the island she had seen so many times in her imagination.

A few kilometres from the town the road swung inland where the sugar cane fields began. The air had a sweeter smell now. The land here was so flat, irrigated by glistening channels of water, that fields of green cane swaying in the breeze could be seen spreading over miles of land. It was as though she and Philip were travellers on a vast sea of green.

As they passed the fields brown-skinned men and women wearing straw hats stopped their hoeing and weeding to eye them curiously. In some fields where the tallest cane grew men were wielding machetes and as the cane fell it was being bundled by women and thrown into carts.

In the distance the hills, today

covered in a blue haze, towered majestically on the horizon. They looked still and lifeless but Lisa's eyes kept straying to them, wondering what activity was going on cloaked in the lush green forests. And in which particular place her father had met his end.

Philip sensed her thoughts and said, 'They told you what happened, didn't they?'

'Señor Pantero told me it was an ambush up in the hills.' She studied Philip's profile. 'How widespread is the support for these rebels?'

'Amongst the peasants it's almost total,' he replied after a slight pause.

There was silence in the car as she digested this unexpected piece of information. From what she had been told previously she believed the rebels to be an isolated band of outlaws.

'You're surprised,' he said, glancing at her. 'You shouldn't be. The peasants on this island are for the most part extremely poor. Those who work on plantations receive a mere pittance but they can't complain or leave because there is nowhere for them to go and the government, such as it is, doesn't stipulate a minimum wage. The country's natural resources haven't been exploited to the full and since Pantero came to power there hasn't been one new school or hospital.'

'But Señor Pantero explained that to me Philip. He has to spend most of his budget on arms to fight the rebels.'

Philip smiled pityingly. 'Lisa, Pantero has been in power for more than thirty years. The rebels were formed — oh — about five years ago and it is only recently that they have begun to really fight.'

Lisa stared at him belligerently. 'What are you trying to tell me? That the men who killed my father are only peace-loving people who want to learn to read and write?'

'The men who killed your father are butchers Lisa,' he said with unexpected vehemence and then more gently, 'but I am trying to get you to understand the other side of it too.'

'I do understand Philip. Poverty and disease makes people do terrible things. It's abominable that people should have to live like that but I'm sure Señor Pantero understands and is doing his best.'

'Yes he is,' Philip replied and he seemed to relax. 'Don't upset him by mentioning it will you? He has enough on his mind already.'

'Of course I won't mention it.' She turned to look out of the window. 'What on earth is that for?' she asked, espying a stone windmill across a field.

'It's an old sugar mill. They're all over the island. Nowadays we use more modern methods — steam not wind. All the planters at this side of the island share a mill a dozen kilometres from my plantation.' Philip glanced in his driving mirror and slowed down sharply, pulling the car to a halt at the side of the road. Before Lisa had time to question him there was a noise like thunder from behind and half a dozen army lorries trundled past. There was a jeep in front of the lorries and as it flashed past Lisa recognised Luis sitting rigidily beside the driver.

Since the evening of the reception he had reverted to his more circumspect way of addressing her, for which she had been grateful. He gave no sign that he remembered their interrupted encounter and neither did she.

Lisa stared thoughtfully at the back of the last lorry as it disappeared in a cloud of dust. 'Where are they going do you think?'

'Probably to raid a village for hidden arms,' he replied with a frown as he started up the engine once more, 'or to provide reinforcements for one of their garrisons.'

'Do you think there will be civil war Philip?'

'It's inevitable,' he said so calmly that she felt suddenly cold.

'Why do you say that? Is it because this man they call El Salvador is a political mischief-maker fooling a few poor gullible people into believing Shangri-la can be achieved by simply removing Pantero?'

Philip remained calm. 'It is inevitable because of the reasons I mentioned before. You saw that shanty town back there. What other hope have these poor souls of getting out? What was your reaction Lisa? Disgust? Did you want to close your eyes and pretend it wasn't there?'

Lisa stared down at the floor. 'I think I felt compassion. Pity that people have to exist in such a sub-human way.'

'With that attitude Lisa you are already halfway to being a rebel sympathiser.'

★   ★   ★

Mary Bannerman came out onto the veranda, waving as she saw the station wagon approach. The plantation house was a small stuccoed bungalow with its tiled roof built low to form the veranda.

The approach to the bungalow, once they left the road, was through groves of cassia trees, their flowers cascading down in a shower of brilliant gold.

As Lisa got out of the car Mary came forward to greet her, grasping both her hands in welcome.

'What a lovely home you have,' Lisa breathed. 'This is more like an island paradise.'

Mary laughed. 'Come inside and meet Rowena.'

They both waved to Philip who turned the car around and drove off the way he had come. Lisa followed Mary into a tiled hall which served as a dining room as well as a living room. Doors around the hall led to other parts of the bungalow.

Lisa's attention was immediately caught by a little girl of about five who was playing on a rug on the floor. When they entered she had glanced up and smiled shyly before returning to her jigsaw puzzle.

'Rowena,' Mary said, 'come and meet

Miss Meredith.'

The little girl, with golden pigtails, stood up with the unhurried grace of the young and shook Lisa's hand gravely.

'I'm very pleased to meet you Rowena,' Lisa said, a little startled to find such a young child.

'I'm five and a half,' the little girl announced, before returning to her puzzle.

Mary laughed. 'Don't be afraid to be surprised. After being married for more than fifteen years she came as a surprise to us too. Would you like to see the garden before we have tea?'

'I'd love to.'

'Rowena, ask Maria to prepare tea please.'

The little girl obediently got up and trotted across the hall and through one of the doors.

Mary and Lisa went back outside where Lisa quickly donned a pair of sunglasses against the sudden glare.

'I'm quite proud of my garden,' Mary

told her. 'When I came to Santa Angelina as a bride there were few English speaking people here and the estate was badly run down which meant Philip was away a lot, so I consoled myself with the garden.'

'It does you credit,' Lisa murmured, stooping to examine a very fragile purple and yellow orchid.

'We grow all our own fruit and vegetables. I still find it a novelty to be able to pick our own bananas and oranges from a tree in the garden.' They paused in the shade of the feathery leaves and yellow bells of a jacaranda tree. Mary's eyes wandered over the garden. In the distance, between palm trees, Lisa caught sight of the sea, shimmering in the sun. 'It was all quite different when the Rodriguez family lived here.'

Lisa turned sharply. 'Rodriguez?'

'Yes, didn't you know? Miguel's family owned this plantation before Philip. When Miguel's father died it was in a pretty run down condition. The crop hadn't been very good for some years and prices were depressed. Philip was looking for a plantation to buy at that time and he bought it from Señora Rodriguez and she went off to America with Miguel to live with her sister. Ah,' she said glancing over Lisa's shoulder, 'I think Maria is bringing out the tea.'

It seemed incongruous to Lisa that she was sitting on the veranda of a bungalow on a beautiful tropical island eating a very English tea and drinking from Spode china tea cups.

'We have a great many of our things sent from England,' Mary explained and then peering down the drive, 'Oh, here comes Philip.'

Philip hurried out of the station wagon and sprinted up the veranda steps. 'I shall be out for my tea later,' he said without pausing, 'Miguel is on his way here.'

It was only a minute or two later that a mud-splattered Land-Rover stopped behind Philip's station wagon and with a distinct feeling of discomfort Lisa watched Miguel get out. He did so slowly and without the sprightliness of Philip who was considerably older. As he came up the steps she was shocked to see how tired he looked.

'*Buenas tardes*' he said with a weary smile that held no mockery or antagonism. Lisa returned the smile and Mary said gently, 'Come and join us for a cup of tea when you're finished.'

'I shall be happy to,' he replied, ruffling Rowena's hair as he passed her chair.

'He works very hard,' Mary said when he had gone in.

'Yes, so I understand.'

'The trouble is he would like to cut himself into twenty pieces and be in twenty different places at once. And to be quite honest it would be a very good thing if he could.' She smiled brightly. 'And how do you like staying at La Casa des flores?'

'It's very comfortable — Inés and her father have been very kind but I can't impose on them for much longer.'

'You intend to return home then?'

'No,' she said with a firmness that surprised her. 'I want to stay here.'

'You know there is always a place for you here Lisa.'

Lisa's eyes suddenly misted over. 'That's very kind of you.'

Mary refilled their cups and handed a slice of toast to her daughter who was quietly leafing through a picture book. 'I don't think Señor Pantero will be anxious to let you leave while you're on the island,' she said.

Lisa frowned, 'I don't understand what you mean Mary.'

Mary seemed to be considering something very carefully before she said, 'It's just that I think he feels responsible for you because of your father. Anyway you and Inés are company for each other.'

'I don't see much of her, but we do get on well enough.'

Mary looked thoughtful again and then said, 'Philip and I were discussing you the other evening. It seems providential that you have a teaching certificate. You see Rowena is going to England to school when she is eight but we have a problem with regard to her education until then. We had some text books sent out but I don't seem to have the knack of getting through to her. We could send her to a school here — she speaks Spanish fluently — but that means school in England will be completely alien to her when she does go . . . '

'And you were wondering if I could give her lessons?'

'Would you Lisa? We'd pay of course.'

Lisa smiled. It was the answer she had been unconsciously seeking. She knew she could not endure a life of idleness indefinitely. 'I'd be delighted to Mary. It will make me feel less useless. I've been wondering what I can usefully do to justify my existence. But on one condition only . . . '

'Anything. Just ask,' Mary said eagerly.

'You're not to offer payment. A good cup of tea is payment enough after all the coffee I've consumed since I left England, and I'm not in desperate need of money. Rafael has heard from Daddy's London solicitors and it seems he managed to save quite a comfortable sum during his lifetime. It's all mine now.'

'Well in that case it's a bargain,' Mary laughed. 'And don't forget what I said about staying here. We'd love to have you.' She turned to Rowena. 'Did you hear that Rowena? Miss Meredith is coming to give you lessons.'

'Will I be able to read *stories*?' she asked eagerly.

'In no time at all,' Lisa replied.

Maria came out onto the veranda with a fresh tray of tea, followed by Philip and Miguel. Miguel always had the effect of making Lisa feel very self-conscious and she lapsed into silence, looking across the colourful garden and the sea in the distance beyond.

'Philip,' Mary said excitedly the moment they appeared, 'Lisa has agreed to teach Rowena. Isn't that marvellous?'

Lisa looked up to smile at him as he replied, 'It certainly is. Thank you Lisa.'

Miguel looked from one to the other before saying, 'What is this?'

'Lisa is going to teach Rowena for a few hours each day,' Philip explained, and it annoyed Lisa that he should have to do so. Philip gave a harsh laugh, 'It will keep her out of mischief don't you think?'

The two men stared hard at each other for a moment and then Miguel said, 'You are right.'

Lisa noticed the lines of fatigue on his face and did not have it in her heart to be really angry at his obvious disapproval.

'You've been at the village this afternoon Miguel?' Mary enquired, after an awkward silence of some seconds.

'My visits seem to take longer each

time I come,' he replied. 'You have cosseted your workers too much you know. They complain of the most trivial illnesses these days.'

'Would you prefer conditions to be like other plantations?' Mary bantered.

'Heaven forbid,' he replied grimly.

Philip finished his tea and stood up, stretching lazily. 'Well, it's back to work for me,' he said. 'Perhaps you would run Lisa back to town for me seeing you're going that way.'

There was an infinitesimal pause before he said, 'Of course.' Lisa was tempted to refuse but to do so would force Philip to take her back and she could not inconvenience him for a childish whim. She would have to be Miguel's unwanted passenger.

'We'll see you again soon Lisa,' Philip said as he prepared to leave. 'Mary will make arrangements for you to come and either one of the boys or myself will collect you from town.'

Miguel also stood up, but before he could say anything Maria came out.

'There is a telephone call for Dr. Rodriguez,' she said.

He excused himself and when he had gone Mary turned back to Lisa. 'I noticed, the other evening, Luis Baldera was very attentive towards you.'

Lisa flushed at the memory of his unwelcome attentions. 'He is just trying to make me feel more at home I expect.'

Mary laughed. 'You don't have to excuse yourself Lisa. You're very honoured I can tell you. He doesn't normally notice women as such. And he *is* an attractive young man, isn't he?'

Mary's eyes watched her shrewdly and for a moment Lisa was reminded of Mrs. Byer. She replied sharply. 'I'm not a silly young girl Mary. My head won't be turned by a smart uniform.'

'I didn't think you were.' She studied Lisa again. 'You're very much your father's daughter I think.'

Before Lisa could question the meaning of this remark Miguel returned. 'We must leave now Miss Meredith,' he said abruptly.

Mary looked up at him, her eyes anxious. 'An emergency?'

'I'm afraid there has been more trouble. A patrol was ambushed this afternoon. They have just brought two men in seriously injured.'

Lisa gasped. 'But we saw some soldiers on our way here this afternoon.'

She saw his face soften slightly, 'Captain Baldera was not among them.'

He waited for her by the Land-Rover while she did a hasty good-bye to Mary and Rowena and made arrangements to come again. The Land-Rover wasn't the most comfortable vehicle to travel in over the rough, bumpy road. Miguel's glance passed over her bare arms and he said, 'You should carry something to cover your arms. The breeze can become quite cool.'

She rubbed her arms and smiled gratefully. 'I will in future.'

He slowed down and reaching for a blanket from the back handed it to her. It smelt mildly of antiseptic. She draped it across her shoulders. His sudden mellowness and thoughtfulness had the effect of thawing her own reserve a little, especially as she wasn't by nature shy.

She guessed he was frustrated by the lack of medical facilities and was greatly overworked — so often the cause of short temper — and she wondered if she had mistaken it for dislike of her. After all, up until now she had been living a fairly idle and useless life and he was bound to resent it.

She studied the strong outline of his face until he became aware of it and he turned to smile at her. It was completely unexpected and unlike the way he had smiled at her before. Her heart skipped a few beats and she lowered her eyes, confused at the sudden change in him.

'I didn't realise you knew the Bannermans so well,' she said. 'They were friends of my father too. Did you know him well?'

'Yes I knew him,' he replied non-commitally, his eyes concentrating on the road ahead in an attempt to avoid the deeper ruts and holes. 'Did you know the Bannerman's plantation belonged to my father at one time?'

'Yes Mary did tell me.' The fields around them were a moving sea of green and as they passed some of the workers stopped to grin and wave their straw hats.

'Did she also tell you after my mother paid all our debts there was no money left so Philip paid our fares to New York and made himself responsible for my education?'

Lisa looked at him in surprise. 'No she didn't.'

'In America education is available to all but I can never repay him enough for making life easier for my mother.'

'They are very nice people,' she said, feeling it was an inadequate statement.

'So,' he continued, in what she considered unusual candour, 'I repay him in the only way I know how — providing medical treatment for his workers. All he has to provide are the drugs.'

'Don't all plantation owners provide the same?'

A bitter smile played around the corners of his mouth. 'That means dipping into their pockets and why should they when there are a hundred other workers ready to step in when one dies or leaves?'

'I'm beginning to learn things about Santa Angelina that I don't very much like.'

He gave a harsh laugh. 'Paradise is not so perfect eh?' Then he became serious once more. 'It is a fact of life out here. The peasants know no different. Privation is not shocking to them, simply a way of life.'

'It shouldn't be.'

'I agree.'

'Do you know if the wounded men are soldiers or rebels?'

Miguel's lips were compressed into a grim line. 'I was not told but I know they will be soldiers. Rebels are never

110

brought to the hospital.'

They were passing the shanty town and her eyes were drawn compellingly towards it. Most of the shacks looked about to collapse and the same nauseating smell filled the air.

The road into Alhaja de mar began to climb and when they stopped outside the gates of La Casa des flores Lisa experienced the same feeling of disappointment she had when the music had stopped during her dance with him.

The gates swung open and they drove in. Luis' jeep was standing in the courtyard and the driver was waiting beside it. Miguel glanced over it briefly and returned his attention to Lisa who slipped the blanket from around her shoulders and handed it back.

'Many thanks for the use of the blanket and the ride.'

For a mere second or two his eyes bored into hers; her throat felt dry and it seemed an interminable time before he said, 'It was a pleasure señorita.' As she turned to go he added with a wry grin, 'If you are ever near the hospital drop in. I think there is a certain lady who may have given you the wrong impression. It is neither a butcher's shop or a chamber of horrors.'

Lisa laughed despite her embarrassment for Mrs. Byer who seemed to be quite notorious.

As he turned the Land-Rover in the courtyard Lisa hurried up the steps, still smiling happily. Today she had seen an entirely different Miguel Rodriguez — and a much nicer one. Was anyone on this island quite what they seemed?

When she reached the door Luis Boldera came hurrying out. His cool glance took in Lisa and Miguel before he said menacingly, 'So, he has returned at last.'

It was an uncomfortable sensation watching him as he hurried into the courtyard. 'Where have you been?' she heard him demand, deciphering his rapid Spanish.

'I came as soon as I heard,' Miguel replied, calmly. 'Your men are already receiving expert help and Dr. Lim assures me there is no immediate danger to either of them.'

'They both have multiple bullet wounds,' Luis Baldera snapped. 'If either one dies because you were out cosseting peasants you will be held personally responsible.'

Miguel ignored his last remark and with one glance at Lisa he accelerated and drew away. Lisa turned into the house with a heavy heart; she had just seen Luis at his officious worst and the look Miguel had given her was as full of dislike as ever before.

5

The following morning started with a torrential shower but by the time Lisa stepped into la plaza the sun was high in the sky and the ground was completely dry. The large square seemed to have shrunk in size owing to the great number of people now packed into it. It was mostly women who were selling their goods, advertising their wares in a cacophony of raucous voices.

Lisa laughingly pushed her way through a crowd of goats being led across the square, resisting pleas to buy goods from the various vendors. It seemed that everyone had brought his or her donkey too, which didn't help the congestion. Not only were people selling but the market had attracted dozens of beggars and they were all so thin that she could not refuse a few pesos to all those who asked.

She paused for a few minutes to watch an old man deftly weaving straw mats and baskets. When he had finished a large mat he held it out to Lisa who could not resist his plea. She handed over the amount he had asked, aware that she was probably paying far too much.

The noise round her was incredible; everyone was intent on talking at the same time and as loudly as possible. The discordant sound of voices mingled with the noise of car horns bent on the impossible task of cleaving a path through the thronging crowd. One thing she was fast learning was the islanders' inherent disrespect for anything mechanical.

As she wandered around, eagerly absorbing everything with her eyes, she became aware of a very noticeable hush that descended on each little section of la plaza as she passed. She was eyed curiously, almost with hostility, and as she passed on the babble began again. No doubt, she decided, it was because she was obviously a stranger.

The rain had done little to keep down the dust caused by so many people in the square and soon her throat was feeling dry. There were several cantinas nearby but they seemed crammed with men and instinctively Lisa knew she should not enter one on her own. She walked along the rows of fruit and vegetables set out on straw mats on the ground. The owners of the merchandise squatted by their mats talking loudly to one another, pausing only to bargain with a customer or in some cases — oblivious to all other noise — singing lustily. Skinny fowls beat their wings helplessly against the bamboo cages in which they were imprisoned and in one corner of la plaza the herd of goats had been tethered. One negress thrust a length of gaudy cotton under her nose but Lisa just laughed and shook her head.

She was about to return to La Casa des flores when she heard a familiar voice behind her. She turned to see Rafael Jeron, immaculately dressed in a shantung suit, bargaining for a length of scarlet silk. She watched from a distance until the vendor gave in and then she sauntered up to him. 'That made into a shirt will make you the most striking man in town!'

His dark eyes danced. 'You think so?' He held it up against him. 'It will make a nice dress for my Consuela, yes?'

'It will suit her very well. She's a lucky woman Rafael to have such a thoughtful husband.'

He handed over his money to the satisfied vendor and began to move away. 'I am a terrible husband and do you know why? Because I am sorry this country does not permit polygamy.'

Lisa laughed, not put out in the slightest by his bantering, knowing the lawyer to be devoted to his beautiful Consuela. They paused beside an old man with a pile of green coconuts. 'It is true Lisa. I have lost my heart to you. If I cannot marry you I am determined you shall marry one of my friends and stay here for ever where I can, at least, look at you. But for the moment I can buy you a coconut to show my devotion.'

He handed over the money and the old man picked up a coconut, deftly slicing off the top with a lethal-looking machete before handing it over. 'A pleasant and cool drink.'

'You must be a mind reader,' she said, taking it gratefully.

As she drank the milk he said, 'It is a much better drink when laced with rum but unfortunately I have none with me.'

Lisa finished the milk and handed back the empty shell. '*Muchas gracias*' she said with a laugh. 'See how my Spanish is improving.' She turned, hearing an excited babble nearby and saw a group of men huddled in a circle. 'What on earth are they up to?' she asked. 'If I were in England I would be sure they were practicing a rugby scrum.'

'It is no football they have in the centre *belleza*, he replied with his usual gusto. 'Those men are enjoying a cockfight.'

Lisa's face crumpled with distaste. 'Ugh!'

He took her arm and escorted her well away from the area. 'Reluctantly I must leave you now. Don José is coming to see me. We shall see you on Saturday at the beach barbecue. *Hasta luego.*'

'*Adios.*' She watched him disappear into the crowd before looking thoughtfully around her, wondering if she had seen everything; there wasn't a great variety of merchandise — there were several of each kind of stall.

Suddenly she caught sight of a young man leaning against a wall. He seemed to be watching her but the moment she looked at him he pulled his ragged straw hat further down over his eyes. What caught her attention and tugged at her heart was the sight of his legs, twisted and crippled as he leaned heavily on a pair of crudely constructed crutches.

Realising it was rude to stare so

blatantly she turned away and began to move across the square, running the gauntlet of demanding voices and pieces of fruit being hopefully thrust at her. In the middle of la plaza there was even a man squatting down by an old sewing machine.

She moved in the direction of the convent, wondering if it was open to public view. La Casa des flores was such a beautiful house she longed to visit the other buildings in Alhaja de mar that had been there since the early days of settlement. So far she had only glimpsed the roof above the high wall.

The solid wooden gates were firmly shut. Lisa turned around in disappointment. The crippled young man was making his way towards her in an awkward way. When he was just in front of her he stumbled and instinctively she rushed forward to catch him as he fell heavily knocking her hand back against the wall. His crutches clattered to the ground.

'*Los siento mucho señorita*,' he murmured.

Lisa held onto him while someone handed him his crutches and put them in position. He repeated his apology and hobbled back into the crowd. Lisa watched him go before realising something was clutched in her hand. Blood seeped slowly out of a graze on the back of her hand where it had been scraped along the wall when he had fallen, but she ignored it, unfurling her fingers to expose a scrap of paper.

She opened it curiously and gasped at the few printed words written on it. YOUR FATHER WOULD WANT YOU TO LEAVE SANTA ANGELINA. She stared at it unbelievingly and as she heard the gate scraping open she stuffed it into her pocket although she was not sure why she did so.

Lisa was taken aback when she saw it was Miguel Rodriguez who had opened the gate. 'I saw you from one of the windows,' he said.

She glanced upwards and then back

to him, not able to stifle a grin of amusement. 'But Dr. Rodriguez what are *you* doing in the *convent*?'

His face was inscrutable. 'Didn't you know? I come here to meditate.' He smiled at her blatant disbelief. 'I am merely teasing. I thought you were just being coy. This is the hospital.' He seized her hand. 'You have been hurt. Come inside and I will dress it for you.'

She snatched her hand back as if she had been stung. 'It's nothing.'

'Come in anyway and have a cup of coffee with me.' He drew her inside and closed the gate. She didn't pause to wonder why he was making a great deal of fuss over what was a very superficial wound.

She found herself in a small court-yard surrounded by a cloistered walk. Their footsteps were loud on the cobbles as they crossed to the main building, passing several nuns in spotlessly white habits. 'It is no longer feasible for the order to be a worship-ping one only,' he explained. 'Most of the sisters are trained nurses which is a blessing in itself.'

He led her up an open stone staircase and along a covered balcony lined with beds. The patients eyed them silently as they passed. Inside the building he led her through several other wards crowded with beds. All the wards were bleak and functional and Lisa could well imagine Mrs. Byer's dismay at having to share a ward with a couple of dozen other people. Their progress seemed to be taking them through the entire hospital. Men smiled and exchanged a word with Miguel as they passed, the women too, and the children watched them shyly with appealing large brown eyes. Lisa wondered if it was a deliberate ploy so that she could see the entire place for herself — in case she had believed Mrs. Byer's ramblings.

'It is ironic don't you think,' he said, encompassing the wards with one hand, 'that these people have to be ill before they have their first decent meal or even sleep in a proper bed for the first time?'

He led her into a tiny room which must have been a nun's cell at one time. The only articles of furniture were an ancient and scarred desk littered with papers and two chairs.

'Please be seated Miss Meredith. I shall be back in one moment.'

Lisa sat down slowly, her mind returning to the scrap of paper the cripple had slipped into her hand. What could it mean? Her father had sent for her to come. Why should he have wanted her to leave? Was it a warning or advice?

The door opened again and Miguel returned — this time carrying a tray and wearing a white coat. She watched him as he poured antiseptic into a bowl of water and glanced down at the blood which had now congealed on her skin.

'It's hardly worth the bother.'

'I do not agree with that.' He took hold of her hand, which was trembling slightly, and dabbed the graze gently with antiseptic on cotton wool. Lisa winced and he said, 'I am sorry if I'm hurting you.'

There was a knock at the door and a girl in a white overall entered carrying two cups of coffee on a tray. The girl eyed Lisa curiously before smiling broadly. Miguel paused to smile at her and say in Spanish, 'Thank you Teresa. That will be all for now.'

The girl went out again and he said to Lisa, 'There is no real need to put a dressing on this but I will put one on just the same.' He smiled at her. 'It is best you should have a reason for being here.'

'Do I need one?' she asked.

He pressed the plaster into place and handed her a cup of coffee before sitting down behind the desk. 'No particular reason I assure you. What do you think of my hospital?'

Lisa sipped at her coffee, reflecting on how she should answer. He would not, she was sure, appreciate uncalled for admiration. 'I think you've done very well within the limitations,' she said carefully after a while. 'Obviously it isn't as good as a hospital in say England or America.'

He was watching her carefully as she spoke. 'I know. I have worked in some very modern hospitals in America.' He looked as though he was about to say something else but he finished his coffee instead. Lisa finished hers and put the cup back on the tray.

'Did you see that man fall?' she asked suddenly.

'Yes.' He began to shuffle some papers around his desk. She knew she should go as he obviously didn't want to talk about it but perversely she insisted. 'What is his name?'

He glanced up at her. 'Why do you want to know?'

'I just wondered that's all. Was he born like that?'

'No,' he snapped.

She leaned forward eagerly. 'So you do know him.'

'Slightly,' he replied without looking at her. 'I know a great many people.'

'It's a great pity such a young man is so badly handicapped.'

He slapped the papers down on the desk and looked at her coldly. 'He does not need your pity Miss Meredith.'

Lisa jumped to her feet; he blurred in front of her eyes. 'I don't know what you have against me Dr. Rodriguez and I don't really care, just as long as you stop blowing hot and cold because I can't stand it.' Her hand closed over the note in her pocket and as quick as a flash she drew it out and threw it across to him. 'I've no doubt you have something to do with this!'

He read it for what seemed an eternity and then he demanded harshly, 'Where did you get this?'

'It was in my hand after that man fell against me. He must have put it there.'

His eyes narrowed thoughtfully for a moment and then he looked up at her. 'I didn't send it. Why should I?'

She knew then he hadn't; he was far more likely to tell her to her face than send an anonymous note. She sank back into the chair. 'Then who *would* send it?'

'Perhaps some young lady who is jealous of your social success.'

She stared hard at him. 'You really do have a bad opinion of me. You'd think men were queueing at the door just hoping for one glimpse of me.'

To her surprise he threw back his head and laughed. 'I think, Miss Meredith, it is you who has the bad opinion of *me*,' he said when he had stopped laughing and then he said more soberly, 'You seem to think I dislike you but it is not true. Nothing is further from the truth I assure you.'

She raised her eyes to meet his and her breath caught in her throat. She stumbled awkwardly to her feet. 'I must go. I've taken up enough of your valuable time as it is.'

He leaned across the desk and caught her wrist. 'No, please don't go just yet. We must not part with a misunderstanding. I admit at first I did think you had come here believing we were a mini-Bermuda, but you did, didn't you?'

She sat down for yet the second time and smiled sheepishly, nodding her head.

'And now you know differently do you still want to stay?'

'Yes I do,' she answered firmly, and wondered, not for the first time, why she was so determined.

He was studying her in the way that disturbed her so much and then he said abruptly. 'You wanted to know about Paco — the man outside . . .'

'You do know him then?' she said hopefully.

'Yes but I *do not* know who gave him this note.'

'I can ask him. He will tell me surely.'

'No he will not. You would be wasting your time asking him.' He stood up and walked over to the window, staring out for a moment or two before turning back to face her. 'You say you want to stay in this country. Well I agree with the writer of the note. You should leave

— go back to England, the country you know.'

'It seems I'm not the most popular person on this island at the moment,' she said dryly. 'I *do* think it's time I went. I'm beginning to realise I've outstayed my welcome.'

'No you will not go until I have told you something.' She looked at him in surprise and he went on. 'I first knew Paco three years ago. He was as normal as you or I. Then one day he was arrested for being a member of the rebel army. He was taken to the prison up at el alcazar for questioning. When they released him he was like that.'

When he had finished speaking there was absolute silence. Lisa closed her eyes tightly but his voice still echoed in her ears. 'It can't be true,' she said, shaking her head as if to convince herself more than anyone else.

'It is true,' he said quietly, watching her carefully from beneath long dark lashes.

She shuddered. 'It's horrible. When I

tell the president . . .'

'You will tell no-one!' His voice shocked her into temporary silence.

'But I must. Don't you see? It can't be allowed to happen again. The men responsible will have to be brought to justice.' She pushed her chair back. 'I must go now. Something must be done for that poor man.'

In a flash he was round to her side of the desk gripping her arms so tightly that she winced. His eyes flashed angrily. 'You will tell no-one! Do you hear Lisa? No-one. Do you know who was in charge of the prison? Baldera. And do you know who gives him his orders? Pantero. And the orders are, find out who the rebels are whatever the cost. Don't be a fool Lisa, Paco has not been the only one.'

The tears she had fought so desperately welled up in her eyes and spilled onto her cheeks. 'How can you condone such a thing?'

He loosened his grip on her but he still did not let her go. 'I condone it?

131

How can you think so? But I am not an impulsive fool. Where would this hospital be without a surgeon?'

Her eyes mirrored her amazement. 'They wouldn't put you in prison surely?'

He smiled without amusement. 'They arrest anyone sympathising with the rebels in the hope that someone will give them a clue to the leader's identity. You cannot blame them; it is their way. That is why I advised you to go home. Your country has a different system and who can say which is right? Every country has its secret police — even yours. Luis Baldera is Captain of the President's Personal Guard, but that is just another name for the man responsible for internal security. Every country has its laws and they must be obeyed; those who do not obey them must be made to — even though those laws and the methods of enforcing them may be alien to some of us. To those who have never lived outside Santa Angelina our laws are not so strange.'

Lisa pulled herself free and fumbled

for her handkerchief. 'It still seems incredible that Luis . . . ' she blushed, 'Captain Baldera should be involved in such an unspeakable crime and Señor Pantero should actually sanction it. I'm sure you must be mistaken.'

He gazed down at her and the sympathy she read in his eyes hurt. 'I am truly sorry,' he said.

A new thought suddenly entered her head and she looked at him sharply. 'My father . . . ' she began.

He shook his head. 'Major Meredith was in charge of training the army and he had nothing to do with Pantero's personal police force.'

'Thank heavens,' she breathed. 'Can anything be done for Paco?'

He moved away from her, back towards the desk but she could still feel the pressure of his hands on her arms. 'It could, but it would take a specialist in orthopaedics and there are none on this island. To send him elsewhere would cost money. Every bone needs to be re-broken and re-set and it is a lengthy business.'

There was a knock on the door and a man Lisa had no difficulty in recognising as Dr. Lim came in. He bowed politely to her and turned immediately to Miguel. 'Dr. Rodriguez will you come please? Private Dejerra is not responding well. The bullet will have to be removed after all.'

'I shall be along immediately.' Dr. Lim bowed once more and went out. Miguel turned to Lisa. 'One of the ambushed soldiers still has a bullet in his head. I was reluctant to remove it as it will be a very delicate task. But now it looks as though it is inevitable. As you see matters are not all one-sided.'

Lisa gathered up her belongings and he said as they left the tiny room, 'I am sorry I had to upset you.'

They walked down the stone corridor. 'I'd much rather know, even if I don't like what I hear. If I want to stay here for any length of time it's as well I face facts. I shall have to learn to respect the president and Captain

Baldera for what they are. As you say laws in every country are different and they're only strange to foreigners.'

He stopped by the staircase. 'You will not mention our conversation.' He lifted her hurt hand, 'Just your injury if anyone asks.'

She smiled reassuringly. 'I won't say a word.'

'Good. El Presidente would be hurt if he thought you disapproved his methods. It is fear of real trouble that makes him so desperate.'

'Goodbye and thank you for the coffee.'

She was aware he was still watching her as she went down the stairs. Her mind was in a turmoil, mostly questioning the loyalty of Miguel Rodriguez. Was he the kind of man who split his loyalty so that he was in favour with both sides? Somehow she doubted it but there was no other answer. He was a trusted friend of Señor Pantero, possibly his future son-in-law, yet she sensed his compassion lay very squarely with the people he cared for so diligently.

As she let herself out of the convent grounds she gazed up at the brooding presence of el alcazar. She found it hard to adjust to the idea of such blatant brutality so close at hand. Miguel had been quite philosophical about it; it was part of life in Santa Angelina just as throwing Christians to the lions had been in Ancient Rome. In many ways Santa Angelina was well behind the times and perhaps it was still backward in the way it adminstered justice. But despite her reasoning and the allowances she made for the difficult political climate Lisa knew she would never get used to it.

She closed the gate with one backward glance, wondering which window was his and over and above the terrible knowledge that had come to her that afternoon was the guilty pain of pleasure within her, because he had called her Lisa.

Inés noticed the plaster the moment

they went into dinner. A prudent streak prevented Lisa from telling her exactly how it had happened. Miguel's earnest entreaty not to mention Paco had affected her more than she realised at the time. On seeing the president this evening she could not really believe he was fully aware of what was going on up at el alcazar. If Señor Pantero was innocent then Luis must be the guilty one and she shrank from that alternative too; yet she believed Miguel implicitly.

'Someone bumped into me,' she replied, 'and I hurt my hand on a wall.'

'Clumsy oaf,' the president remarked, his mouth full of food.

Lisa pushed her food around her plate, every time she remembered Paco a flood of revulsion washed over her and she could not eat.

'It has been expertly dressed,' Inés remarked.

Lisa could not meet her eyes; she was angry at her own feeling of guilt and more than uncomfortable about the obscure reason for it. She mumbled, 'Dr. Rodriguez saw it happen and took me into the hospital.'

Inés's lips tightened a fraction as she said, 'How fortunate.'

The president wiped his greasy lips on his napkin and said, 'You must have met many people in the square today.'

Lisa looked at him suspiciously but his plump face was as bland as ever. 'I met Señor Jeron buying some silk for his wife and of course Dr. Rodriguez.'

'The market is quite different from anything you have ever seen before, is it not?'

Lisa managed to laugh. 'Oh yes.' She winced as she accidentally knocked her hand on the edge of the table and was surprised to find it was trembling.

The president did not miss her grimace and he said sharply. 'Something will have to be done about that fool Paco.'

Lisa's fork dropped onto her plate and she had the impression that Inés had caught her breath. 'Paco?'

Jorge Pantero spread his hands in a helpless gesture, smiling sheepishly. 'It could be no-one else. It happens all the time.'

Lisa was filled with the dismaying thought that one of those bland faces in la plaza that afternoon had been watching every move she made. She quickly recovered from her shock and boldly pressed on. 'Whilst I was at the hospital Dr. Rodriguez was called to one of the men injured in the ambush yesterday.'

The president looked sad. 'Ah yes. A young man, newly married. The operation was carried out this afternoon. Even if he recovers he will never be the same. It is so sad. It is ironic is it not that the bullets come from our own guns stolen by the outlaws at the cost of my soldiers' lives. They seem to know exactly when we are moving arms. They even drive away our trucks and jeeps after slaughtering the occupants. If only we could discover the ringleaders there would be no more bloodshed and good men like your father would not perish uselessly. We live in difficult times,' he added with an expressive sigh.

Lisa stared down at her plate. 'No rebels were brought in for treatment.'

There was a steely glint in the president's eyes. 'When one of them is injured the others drag him away so he will not be captured. They are cowards Lisa and if they are captured would immediately throw themselves on my mercy, so their comrades dare not leave them, and they have to go without medical help. It is unfortunate.'

Señor Panterno's account did not tally with Miguel's, but Lisa realised just then she could no longer take anything anyone said at face value. She was determined to remain on the island but she knew it was imperative for her to leave La Casa des flores and as she glanced across at Inés' beautiful face she realised it was for more than one reason.

'You are not eating Lisa,' Inés broke in hastily, 'perhaps you have done too much today. You must take life easy for the next few days so that you will be fresh for the barbecue on Saturday.'

Lisa pushed her plate away and looked at the president.

'Inés is correct Señor Pantero. May I go to my room and rest?'

'Of course my dear. You must take care of yourself.'

As she closed the door behind her she was aware of his speculative stare as she left the room.

6

No-one bothered to cross their fingers for the weather to keep fine for the barbecue; apart from the occasional tropical storms — which were brief and dried up immediately — the sun shone almost continuously. Now she was more used to the constant heat Lisa loved it. It was never too hot; an ever-present breeze cooled the island and whispered through the feathery fronds capping the coconut palms which seemed to grow everywhere.

The plan was for the barbecue to be held on a beach at the other side of the island and as the roads were poor it was arranged for the party to travel by boat around the island. Inés and Lisa travelled down to the harbour in the president's limousine escorted by Luis Baldera, looking strange in an ordinary sweater and slacks. Lisa couldn't imagine him being ruthless or cruel when he was not in uniform but she guessed that he himself was feeling slightly uncomfortable without his holster and pistol.

He behaved very correctly towards both girls which caused Lisa to sigh with relief, hoping the episode in the garden could be put down to a momentary lapse on his part.

Rafael and Consuela Jeron were waiting for them on the wharf beside the president's sleek white cabin cruiser and they waved gaily on seeing the three latest arrivals. Lisa recognised most of the other young people who were also waiting on the wharf; they had been at the reception and were mainly Luis' army colleagues with their wives and girl friends and there were also several sons and daughters of plantation owners present too.

'Now you have arrived,' Rafael announced, 'we can depart.' He waved the others to the boat in an authoritative way.

Luis and Rafael climbed onto the cruiser's deck and helped the women down. Lisa waited until Inés and Consuela were on board and then Luis gripped her firmly round the waist to lift her down. Once on the deck of the boat he made no move to let her go; he kept hold of her waist and smiled mockingly into her eyes. She pulled herself free and went over to where Rafael, Consuela and Inés were talking.

The engine spluttered into life. The pilot cast off and the cruiser edged smoothly out into the wide bay.

The breeze bit against Lisa's face bringing tears to her eyes and streamed her hair out behind her. The girls tied scarves around their heads and shrugged into heavy cardigans while the men pulled sweaters over their thin shirts. Lisa had taken special care getting ready that morning, choosing her prettiest and newest dress of the palest blue with a scooped neck and full skirt.

She watched the harbour recede and

then turned and went into the cabin furnished with plush chairs and a cocktail cabinet. She hardly knew whether it was relief or disappointment she felt because Miguel Rodriguez had not come.

She sat in the cabin staring out to sea. The boat was following the line of the coast. A few minutes later Inés came in and pulled the scarf from her hair.

'You should really come on deck Lisa; it is very invigorating.'

'In a few minutes,' she replied. 'Sit down with me Inés, I want to talk to you.'

Inés, her eyes alight with curiosity, complied and Lisa said, 'You know I'm giving Rowena Bannerman lessons?'

'Yes,' Inés smiled. 'I think it is a good idea. It will keep your mind away from more unpleasant things.'

Lisa twisted her scarf between her fingers. 'It might also be a good idea if I stayed with the Bannermans for the time being.' Something like alarm

145

passed across Inés's face and Lisa went on hurriedly, 'It would be more convenient for Philip you see; at the moment I have to be collected and taken to the plantation and then brought back afterwards.'

Inés stared out of the porthole and then turned to smile at Lisa. 'It must be as you wish Lisa. But let us still be friends. You will still come to see me?'

Lisa smiled with relief, grasping both Ines's hands in her own. 'You know I will.' She hesitated a moment before asking, 'Will your father mind? I thought I would speak to you first. After all you've both been very kind to me since I came and I don't want you to think I'm ungrateful . . .'

'Leave Papa to me Lisa. He understands English well but I can explain to him better than you.' She stood up, looking down at Lisa. 'I am glad you are going, although I will miss your company. It will be better for you at the Bannerman's house.'

Lisa watched Inés go out on deck,

slightly puzzled by that enigmatic statement but because she was so relieved at finding it easier than she imagined it would be to tell Inés, she dismissed it from her mind. After tying a scarf into place she followed Inés on deck. Rafael and Consuela were sitting against the cabin wall. Rafael's arm was loosely round his wife's shoulder as they stared silently out to sea. An aura of unspoken devotion surrounded them and Lisa was reluctant to intrude. At the sight of them sitting so contentedly together her heart constricted. Would she ever share this kind of love? One that was all encompassing.

Luis and the others were standing at the bow end of the cruiser, their backs towards her and she was reluctant to join them too. Rafael looked up and on seeing her waved her over. 'Come and join us,' he shouted. She went over slowly and he tapped the deck. 'Sit down. We have a long journey yet.'

She sank down beside them, her mind far away. While they were on their way to a carefree afternoon at the beach where was Miguel Rodriguez? As the boat skimmed through brilliantly blue waters she wondered how many lives he would save on that same afternoon in his inadequate and airless hospital.

It was early in the afternoon when the cruiser rounded the headland and sailed into calmer waters. The breeze dropped, the temperature soared and soon they were stripping off their sweaters and cardigans.

The cruiser hugged the coast until they sailed into a small cove. The beach was exactly as she imagined it would be — silver white sand fringed with towering palms. They sailed the full length of the cove, past the small stuccoed bungalow belonging to the Bannermans. There was a small village at the edge of the cove — little wooden huts with thatched palm leaf roofs — and the cruiser tied up at last at a rickety pier.

The women and children of the village, dressed in bright cotton dresses, were mending fishing nets on the beach when the party stepped ashore. This time, to Lisa's relief, it was Rafael who helped her from the boat. His light-hearted flirting was far preferable to her than Luis's sly innuendoes.

The villagers laughed and chattered in an unfamiliar patois and pointed delightedly to Lisa's hair.

'They rarely see hair so fair,' Rafael whispered.

The women allowed the villagers to crowd around them examining their clothes and hairstyles with great interest and amusement. Finally they were drawn away by the men and as they walked across the powdery sand, so incredibly white it dazzled Lisa's eyes, she slipped off her sandals and enjoyed the luxury of going barefoot.

Philip's bungalow was almost a replica in miniature of their plantation house. When they reached it the rest of them waited in the welcome shade of the veranda while Rafael and Luis went inside to return a few minutes later carrying trays of iced rum punch.

Most of the other young people present spoke a little English and between them they managed to keep Lisa in conversation. None of them had been to England and they were naturally curious and questioning. Sitting on the veranda gazing across an expanse of silvery blue sea lapping gently against the white sands and surrounded by pleasant company, normally Lisa would have been more than contented, but today, knowing the unrest amongst the poorer people on the island, she could not relax fully. And at the back of her mind there was the vague uneasy feeling that there was something very important missing from her life.

Rafael suddenly clapped his hands together and silence fell. Everyone looked towards him expectantly. He was not very tall but with his dark eyes sparkling brightly Lisa was forced to admit to herself that his very presence commanded attention and she was amazed to see how readily the others allowed him to take control of the operation.

'We have all day in which to enjoy ourselves,' he said, 'but it is pleasant for swimming now. You ladies can use the bungalow first while we men set up the spit.'

They were all wearing their swimming costumes underneath their clothes so it was only minutes later when they ran back onto the beach and into the water. Lisa was slightly dismayed and embarrassed to find that she was the only one wearing a bikini; although the other women admired it greatly she was informed that bikinis were not generally worn in Santa Angelina.

The pig was already turning on the spit over a roaring fire. Lisa splashed about in the water near the shore with the others and even Luis, when the men joined them, shared in the fun.

Finally they all swam into deeper water and Lisa turned on her back and floated lazily, staring up at the cloudless sky.

The little bay with its backdrop of palm and flame-capped poinciana trees was as picturesque as anyone could wish. It was as distant from the dirt of Alhaja de mar as a sleepy English country village was from London. She could hardly blame her father for seeking rest and solitude here; away from the terrible possibility of civil strife on the island she knew he had come to love. Surely he must have had some inkling as to the happenings up at el alcazar but what, she wondered, was his reaction. He was a hardened soldier; perhaps he accepted it as part of the way of life here like everyone else seemed to do.

Luis swam up to her. 'You have been in too long Lisa,' he said.

He looked like any other man without his uniform and so utterly harmless that she had to smile. 'Race you to the shore,' she challenged, but she was no match for his powerful and practiced strokes and he was laughing on the beach when she struggled ashore.

He gripped her hand and they ran up the beach. She threw herself weakly onto her towel and lay there panting and laughing until her breathing returned to normal and she was able to sit up once again.

Luis lay on the beach next to her, his head propped on one hand and his eyes, full of undisguised admiration, were on her.

'I could do with a drink,' she said, in an effort to break the embarrassing silence.

He immediately jumped to his feet. 'At your command señorita!'

'And would you bring my beach bag too Luis?'

He turned towards the bungalow and she followed him with her eyes, hoping that he did not intend to renew his amorous advances. At least she could be sure of being fairly safe amongst such a crowd, especially as several of them were his subordinates.

Lisa stiffened suddenly as she saw Luis stop to speak to Rafael and his wife who were standing on the veranda steps, for with them were Inés and Miguel. She blinked her eyes but when she opened them again he was still there; taller and darker than any of them. Luis went on into the bungalow and the two couples strolled down towards the water. Miguel was wearing only a pair of white swimming trunks and against them his skin was deeply bronzed.

Lisa could do nothing but wait for them, unless she wanted to go back into the water, and she didn't. Instead she looked boldly towards them and smiled brightly, shading her eyes with her hand.

'Such a pretty flower and all alone!' exclaimed Rafael, 'but never mind Luis — the lucky dog — will soon return.'

For once Lisa did not find him amusing, but she still smiled because it wasn't his fault she couldn't respond to his jesting just at that moment.

'Will you join us for another swim?' Inés asked, but Lisa knew it was merely politeness; her presence would surely be superfluous.

Before she had chance to reply Miguel said, 'After such a game try to beat Luis I doubt if Miss Meredith will want to swim for a while yet. It was a good try but you had no chance of winning against him.'

Her heart sank on two counts. Firstly he was back to addressing her with his former coolness and secondly to an onlooker she and Luis must have appeared to have been on very intimate terms.

She managed to laugh. 'Thank you for telling me — now. I don't recall seeing you on the boat.'

'Then you won't be surprised to learn I was not on it,' he replied lightly and then more seriously he explained, 'I have been on this side of the island for the past two days. I do occasionally travel around in case someone needs treatment. The country folk are very reluctant to travel into town.' He paused for a moment and then said, 'I see your hand is better.'

Lisa looked down at the almost indiscernable mark and then back to him. 'Yes, it's fine now.' Her face crumpled into a grin. 'I can give Mrs. Byer a testimonial as to your ability if it's ever necessary.'

His answering smile was just for her and she couldn't drag her eyes away from his until Rafael, laughing loudly said, 'Just look at Luis! How I wish I had brought my camera.'

All eyes were turned on Luis and Lisa found it very difficult to suppress a giggle at the sight of the Captain of The President's Personal Guard walking down the beach, her bright plastic beach bag slung across his shoulder and a tall glass of rum punch in each hand.

Miguel looked back to Lisa. 'It is quite amazing what love can do to a man.'

Lisa knew her face suffused with

colour and she was relieved when Inés tugged at his arm saying, 'Let us have that swim now Miguel, before it is too late.' She shot one last worried look at Luis, 'Luis does not like being the object of fun.'

Lisa buried her face in her hunched up knees for a minute or two until the others had gone. Only then did she raise her head to smile at Luis. 'I'm really longing for a drink,' she said as he handed it to her.

He dropped her bag onto the sand beside her and stared fiercely to where Miguel and the others were swimming. 'Jeron is a buffoon. An idiot,' he said.

He sank down onto the sand next to her and she said, 'It's all show Luis. He must have a serious side. He is said to be the best lawyer in Santa Angelina.'

'Ha!' Luis scoffed. 'Rodriguez is supposed to be the best surgeon but on Santa Angelina that is saying very little.' He turned to her then, his face softened by the boyish smile that could trans-form him. 'But I am glad Rodriguez has come; it means I can devote myself to you.'

Lisa moved almost imperceptibly further away a fraction. She sipped at her drink thoughtfully for a moment or two and then said, 'Because we have been thrown together like this doesn't mean you have to devote yourself entirely to me. We *have* come as a party.'

They both glanced around them. Miguel, Inés, Rafael and Consuela were still in the water, others were sunbathing a little way away and two couples were laughing as they attended the barbecue.

Lisa heard a ripple of excitement among the others and followed the direction of their gaze. 'Oh look at that Luis,' she said, glad of a distraction. A young village boy was rapidly climbing a coconut palm with the aid of a looped piece of rope. Once at the top he threw the coconuts down to another boy on the ground who sliced off the tops with his machete and ran round offering them to everyone. Lisa laughingly accepted one and allowed Luis to lace the milk with rum and she had to admit it tasted both delicious and refreshing.

'It is only nature for us to pair off Lisa,' he said when she had finished. 'Most of these people are either married or betrothed and that goes for Inés too.'

She lay back on the sand, closing her eyes, knowing what he said to be true but hating to hear it spoken. A shadow blocked the sun's warmth from her face and she opened her eyes again to see him leaning over her.

'I know you are very modest *querida*. I understand you do not like to admit you are attracted to me. It is the English way I believe.'

She sat up so quickly she almost knocked him sideways in her haste. 'I'm sorry Luis,' she said jerkily. 'I do like you, but nothing more you understand.'

His eyes became cold and she saw the cruel twist to his lips as he said, 'We shall see, yes we shall see.' He gripped her wrist tightly, his face close to her averted cheek. 'There is going to be fighting within these shores before long and a war torn country is never a pleasant place for a woman especially one who is both beautiful and alone. You would do well to cultivate an influential friend — one who would protect you from those who use war as an excuse to seize what they would normally have to ask for.'

'Miss Meredith can hardly eat if you continue to hold her like that.'

With a sharp intake of breath Lisa pulled her hand free at the sound of the familiar voice. Miguel towered over them, droplets of water falling onto Lisa's skin from his dripping body. He stooped to help her to her feet while Luis stared at him, his face contorted with silent rage.

Lisa gathered up her things in the uneasy silence. Just then Inés — completely unaware of the strain between the two men — came running up to them rubbing her long black hair briskly with a towel. 'The food is ready Lisa!' she said excitedly. 'Come and sample your first beach-barbecued pig!'

★   ★   ★

It was already dark by the time the cruiser cleaved its way back to Alhaja de mar. Lisa thought she would remember the sight of the sunset from the beach forever. As the sun sank slowly enflaming the entire sky the fishing boats returned to their village and as the sky turned from crimson to purple the voices of the fishermen could be heard singing their sad shanty. The party on the beach sat on the sand like children at a puppet show, watching the unique spectacle and listening to the heart-stirring refrain.

Luis had remained sullenly apart for the rest of the afternoon and as darkness began to fall Lisa found herself sitting next to Miguel.

'What are they singing about?' she asked in a whisper. He leaned closer and said softly. 'It is a song hundreds of years old. It tells of a sailor far away from his native land who falls in love with a beautiful mermaid. She can only live in the sea so one night, after much heart searching, he hears her singing and he knows he must join her.'

'And do they live happily ever after?'

He laughed softly. 'Oh yes certainly.'

Now the breeze was cool. The others were having coffee in the cabin and Lisa was staring at the reflection of the moon on the rippling sea. She was inwardly restless; depressed, and at the same time elated.

★ ★ ★

The next morning Lisa awoke and the first thing she remembered was her intention to leave La Casa des flores the next day. She also remembered that Inés had insisted she be the one to tell the president, but Lisa knew, after his kindness to her, she would have to tell him herself.

As she dressed her hand trembled a little through nervousness. Even though he had always behaved with fatherly kindness towards her Lisa was aware she was slightly afraid of him, especially after what Miguel had told her.

Miguel. Her hand trembled even more at the thought of him. Why was it he was able to arouse such powerful emotions within her? Had he returned to Alhaja de mar just yet? When they had left the cove the night before he had remained at the bungalow, choosing to stay there for the night and return the next day. For the first time she was beginning to appreciate how hard worked he really was. It was far more preferable for Dr. Lim to travel about the island attending to the peasants' minor illnesses and allow Miguel to remain at the hospital to attend to those who needed surgical treatment, but Lisa had been given to understand that the country and hill people spoke a strange patois that Dr. Lim was unable to understand or speak and therefore Miguel had no alternative but to go.

Lisa smoothed her hair and glanced at her watch. Señor Pantero should be in the salon now; she would be sure to catch him.

An armed sentry guarded each end of the corridor and even though she now appreciated the necessity of their presence she could not help but eye them with a certain amount of trepidation.

She went down the corridor, her sandalled feet making no noise on the tiled floor. As she approached the salon she was about to put her hand out to open the door when the sound of the president's voice, raised in anger, made her pull back.

'You fool!' he cried, 'You calmly agree to her suggestion. What kind of imbeciles am I surrounded with?'

Lisa's ears strained to catch his words. She was vexed at the educational system that made her almost fluent in French and German but left her with only a smattering of Spanish she now needed to know.

When she heard Inés's usually soft voice raised too Lisa was committed to eavesdrop further. 'I am glad she is going, do you hear! Glad she will be away from you and your spies! I am sick of being a spy for you. I told her to go!'

Lisa started violently at the sound of hand meeting flesh and the cry that was wrung from her friend. She had a moment only to shrink into an alcove before the door was wrenched open and Inés — a hand to a livid weal on her cheek and tears streaming down her face — came rushing out.

Lisa's first impulse was to follow and comfort Inés but to do so would only serve as an admission she was listening; she did not doubt that she had been the subject of the angry exchange between father and daughter but she could not imagine why.

In her flight Inés had left the door slightly ajar and Lisa could still hear clearly from the alcove when the

165

president's voice rose again. 'And you,' he cried, 'what excuse for failure have you?'

'None, Your Excellency,' Luis Baldera replied.

'You are an idiot too Baldera. I told you to keep close to her, make her fall in love with you a little if it will make it easier for you. Why not? You are a handsome young man. But no. You have to charge in and make violent love and frighten her away. Ah you make me sick. She is an English girl of breeding not a peasant from the village slums. Do you not know the difference?'

'I admit my failure Your Excellency. My resignation will be on your desk tomorrow morning.'

'Shut up stupid. You are the best soldier I have even if you are the worst lover.'

'I am grateful Your Excellency. I will do my utmost to make amends for this failure.'

'Bring me El Salvador dead or alive, but preferably alive, and I shall be satisfied.'

'I intend to Your Excellency.'

Lisa shrank back further into the alcove at the sound of the menace in his voice; the same sound she had recognised the day before on the beach and she shivered.

She heard Luis cross the floor and then as he stood just inside the door, 'I personally believe the girl is innocent of all knowledge.'

'I too Baldera, but that is not to say they will not contact her.'

'If she is innocent she will soon betray them. Another consignment of small arms have been despatched to Maros this morning Your Excellency. All suspects are under observation.'

'Good. This load must arrive safely. We have lost too much to the rebels already.'

Lisa heard the clicking of his heels and she held her breath as he came out of the salon. She was so near she could reach out and touch him. Any moment he would look up to see her there and guess she had overheard everything. To her relief he turned and marched off in the opposite direction. As soon as she heard the sound of his boots on the hall below she turned swiftly and fled back to the privacy of her room.

She sank down onto the bed, her mind evaluating all she had heard. Why was the president so angry with Inés because she was leaving? And more humiliating why had Luis been ordered to pay his odious attentions to her?

There were so many questions that needed answering, but she could not get them without admitting she had overheard the conversation. And after the harsh sound of Señor Pantero's voice she would hate to do that.

She hardly knew how she would get through the day without giving herself away to either the president or Inés. Worst still she dreaded facing Luis now she knew the mercenary reason behind his pursuit of her. Although, now she considered the matter more closely, somehow she doubted if it was done so unfeelingly; there was something about the way he looked at her that told her there was more to it than that. But she was not reassured; a proud man like Luis Baldera would take a personal slight from her much harder than harsh words from his president.

7

Three months later Lisa sat on the veranda of the plantation bungalow marvelling because the sun was still shining despite the ending of the summer. There was little to indicate the coming of autumn except for the rainstorms becoming less frequent of late.

'Another cup of tea Lisa?'

She brought her mind back and passed her cup over to Mary.

'Tea and toast,' she said, 'it's almost like being in England.'

Mary cast a rueful glance across her colourful garden before handing the refilled cup. 'Hardly. Speaking of England your Spanish has improved tremendously since you came to us.'

'Because of Maria,' she replied, thinking of the cook whose friend she had become. Lisa insisted on conducting all their conversations in Spanish however difficult it had been for herself at the beginning. 'One of these days I'm going to start a school here,' she said wistfully.

Mary laughed. 'Oh good. You can start on our little rascals in the village when you do. If you can teach them as well as you've taught Rowena we'll have them reading and writing in no time.'

'I like the books Aunty Lisa brings me,' Rowena cut in from the veranda floor where she was crayoning a very colourful picture.

'There you are,' Mary said resignedly, 'they're the same books I tried to use.'

'She's intelligent Mary *and* a joy to teach. I had some very tough infants to tame during the teacher training course. This is nothing like work.'

'We've been glad to have you for your own sake Lisa,' Mary said. 'I've enjoyed having you around. It's marvellous to be able to have a real honest to goodness chat without having to choose the simplest words. Consuela is a sweet child but her English vocabulary consists of half a dozen words.'

'And I've enjoyed being here,' Lisa said truthfully. It had been so peaceful at the Bannerman's plantation that quite often she had wondered if she had imagined all the undertones at La Casa des flores. There was no doubt about the conversation she had heard — although she hadn't mentioned it to anyone — but now she wondered if she'd attached too much sinister importance to it. Señor Pantero's fiery Latin temper could easily have been raised because he felt he was not doing enough for the daughter of a man who had died in his service.

Another reason for leaving the town — although one she was reluctant to admit even to herself — was to avoid contact with Miguel Rodriguez and his disturbing influence on her.

She could not forget it was he who had caused her to question everyone's motives. But if she hoped to elude him it was a vain desire; once a week he came to the plantation village to hold a clinic and he always came up to the house afterwards. Not only that, he paid frequent social calls on the Bannermans and once he arrived with Inés in the presidential limousine.

On these occasions his manner towards her was warmer than on previous occasions but nothing like the near intimacy when she visited the hospital. Try as she would she could not dispel the memory of the expression in his eyes and the closeness of his body to hers when he had held her. And somewhat comforting was the revelation that it was only in the company of others that he held himself aloof from her, although the reason for that puzzled her.

During her stay with the Bannermans they had all spent several long weekends at the bungalow at the beach. For Lisa it was as near an idyll as one could get. Much as she enjoyed life on the plantation she wished she could stay at the beach forever.

'How would you like to go down to the village?' Mary asked suddenly.

'Now?'

'Why not? I can't think why I haven't taken you before.'

'Because each time you've been there I have been doing something else.'

'That must be why,' Mary replied, with her ready laugh.

'Won't everyone be working in the fields?'

'No, not now Lisa. When we start harvesting after Christmas all except the tinies and the new mothers will be out in the fields.' She got out of her chair. 'I shall be back in a moment; there are some things I have to get. Shall I fetch your cardigan?'

'Please.' Lisa smiled to herself, knowing the 'things' Mary was fetching were baskets of food for the villagers.

True enough she returned ten minutes later with two large baskets containing fruit and vegetables and a large white box.

'They have their own plots don't they

Mary?' she asked.

'Yes, but extras are always needed. The children eat a lot and never get enough and there are lots of children.'

'And what is in the box?'

Mary grinned and pushed it across the table. 'Take a look.'

A little suspiciously Lisa lifted the lid and gazed down at the tiny garments contained in the box. 'Oh how sweet! Who are they for?'

'I always make a gift of a complete layette for each new baby. The poor little devils wear hand-me-downs for the rest of their lives so I think they should at least start off with something new. I go mad occasionally and knit a load of jackets and then make a dozen dresses. It keeps me busy and I have a pile of garments ready when they're needed.'

Lisa's eyes shone. 'Mary you're marvellous.'

Mary looked away in embarrassment. 'Nonsense. Shall we go? Coming Rowena?'

Rowena shook her head and continued with her crayoning. Mary threw Lisa her cardigan and passed over one of the baskets. 'We'll go across the fields. It's quicker than by road.'

'Who is the layette for Mary?' she asked as they strolled along.

'Manuela — Maria's daughter. She's expecting her first child next month.'

Lisa stared at Mary in surprise. 'Maria's *daughter*! She doesn't look old enough to have a grown up daughter. She can't be much more than thirty.'

Mary smiled wryly. 'Wait until you see Manuela.' She looked at Lisa. 'You've got to keep remembering things are different here. People mature much earlier. To us Manuela is no more than a child but amongst her own people she is a woman. I feel particularly fond of most of these new mothers; I can remember them being born when I was new to this island. They're very grateful for anything that is done for them. The trouble is not enough can be done. We just can't afford to make all the

176

improvements we'd like and the government doesn't help.'

They paused on the brow of a hill and gazed down at the cluster of neat wooden cabins with their corrugated iron roofs, each with it's own piece of land. Further away were the larger buildings belonging to the overseers and beyond them a long barrack type building which she knew was used as a part-time clinic and recreation centre the remainder of the time — the only one of its kind on the island.

As they approached Lisa saw there was a central piece of land alive with skinny chickens, tethered goats and two cows. Small children swarmed everywhere until they caught sight of the two women and they fell silent to stand watching them curiously with appealing dark eyes.

A group of young women, most of them nursing babies in their arms, were standing outside one of the cabins and on seeing Mary and Lisa they too became silent. Mary's smile faded.

'That's Manuela's cabin,' she said and rushed forward to question the women.

They all replied in unison and spoke so quickly and with such a focal accent that Lisa could not follow. Mary put the basket of food down. 'Leave yours here Lisa,' she said quietly, 'these women will distribute the food. Manuela has started to have the baby.'

Lisa put the basket down watched by the silent women and then she followed Mary into the dim interior of the cabin. It consisted of one room only. The walls of plain wood were decorated by cooking utensils and the only furniture was a large mattress on a floor covered by woven palm leaf mats. A crudely carved wooden crucifix hung on the wall over the mattress, on which lay a girl who could be no more than sixteen years old. Her black hair streamed down to her shoulders at either side of her small pale face.

There was another woman near the mattress and she was speaking to Mary in a low whisper. 'Is anything wrong?'

Lisa asked when she had finished.

Mary looked down at the girl and then came across to Lisa. 'I don't know. She's started early but that in itself doesn't really matter.' Manuela began to moan and both Mary and Lisa looked towards her. The older woman had knelt on the floor and was holding Manuela's hand.

'Isabel is the next best thing to a midwife we have. She's seen more babies into the world than most doctors and she has been taught the rudiments of hygiene and how to recognise any danger signals. She says Manuela has been like this since this morning and even allowing for a slow labour she doesn't think it's right. It's very unusual so I can understand her worry; these girls usually have their babies very easily and I'm inclined to trust Isabel's intuition.'

'What are you going to do?' Manuela began to moan again and Mary bit her lip. 'I think I should go back to the house and telephone the hospital. If

179

Miguel can't come Dr. Lim will.' She glanced uneasily at Lisa for a moment and then said, 'Would you stay Lisa? If the baby does come soon you might be able to do something to help Isabel. The other women are hopeless; they just stand and grin when it comes to the crunch.'

Suddenly Lisa felt trapped; she didn't want to be here when Miguel came. Something of the panic she felt must have shown on her face for Mary said, 'If you can't face it forget it. I was forgetting how young you are. I was the same when I first came to the island but it's surprising how quickly I learned. In those days it was a matter of necessity; there were no doctors available and these people hadn't a clue about elementary hygiene. But I still remember how I felt the first few times.'

Lisa realised how selfish she was being. If there was the remotest chance of helping Maria's daughter she must stay and not rush off because of an emotion too nebulous to understand.

'Of course I'll stay Mary,' she said.

'You're sure you don't mind?' Mary asked anxiously.

Lisa gave her a reassuring smile. 'I don't think I will faint if that's what you're afraid of.' She glanced over to Manuela who was watching her with fear-filled eyes. 'When I think what a child *I* was at that age . . . '

Mary patted her arm. 'Thanks Lisa. I shall go now and telephone the minute I get back.' She bent to speak to Isabel who smiled at Lisa and nodded.

After Mary had gone Lisa went over and knelt down by Manuela's head. The girl turned and smiled at her and whispered '*Gracias*'.

Beads of perspiration sparkled on her brow and upper lip and Lisa fumbled in her bag for a handkerchief and the bottle of eau de cologne she always carried. She bathed Manuela's face gently with the moistened cloth. Isabel indicated she was going out for a while and Lisa was a little nervous at being left alone with the girl, although she knew the birth could not be imminent.

Manuela turned to speak to Lisa and she had to bend her head to hear what she was saying. After a moment or two she realised Manuela was asking to see the clothes Mary had brought and she fetched the box over to her. Manuela smiled happily as Lisa held up each garment for her to examine and it came as a revelation to her that as young and as poor as the girl undoubtedly was she was looking forward to the birth of her baby.

Isabel returned, surprisingly with cups of coffee for Lisa and herself and a glass of water for Manuela. After they had finished Lisa bathed Manuela's face again and then sat back to wait. She glanced at her watch frequently; the minutes ticked past with agonising slowness. An hour went by, an hour and a half. Still the girl had spasmodic pains and each time an anxious Lisa glanced hopefully across to Isabel who shook her head grimly.

Lisa soon found the heat inside the

cabin and her own anxiety for the girl was beginning to tell. Perspiration began to run down her own face which she hastily wiped away. She stiffened at the sound of a commotion outside and a moment later in ran a young man, little older than Manuela, who threw himself on the floor by her side babbling almost incoherently as he grasped hold of her hand. This Lisa knew was the young father-to-be and from the way Isabel was remonstrating with him she guessed someone had told him Manuela was dying and her own heart was stricken with fear.

Isabel almost lifted his slight frame bodily from the floor and propelled him through the opening and slammed the door shut behind him. 'I won't have him frightening her,' Lisa managed to interpret.

Both fell silent at the sound of a vehicle stopping outside the cabin. Lisa gave a swift prayer of thanks and sat back on her heels as Miguel rushed into the room. He stopped in his tracks when he saw Lisa, kneeling unexpectedly by Manuela's side and then he said rather breathlessly, 'I am sorry I could not get here sooner.'

Lisa looked down at the girl and was surprised to see the fear had completely gone from her face and she looked relaxed and almost happy. While Miguel questioned Isabel Lisa wiped Manuela's face again with the handkerchief soaked in eau de cologne.

When he had finished he knelt down on the floor and said sharply across Manuela, 'What are you doing here?'

He was angry with her, she knew, but on this occasion she was too concerned about the girl to let it worry her. He turned to Manuela and smiled, and for a second she resented the girl for receiving his favour. He spoke quietly to her for a few moments. She was still smiling when he made a gentle examination. Lisa watched tensely; she only realised how tensely when her nails bit into the palms of her hands. Somehow knowing Maria and seeing this happy girl it was important to Lisa that nothing should go wrong.

When he had finished at last Lisa waited anxiously as he sat back on his heels and then looked at Manuela. 'You will be all right Manuela.'

'And the baby?' she whispered anxiously.

He hesitated a fraction of a second before saying emphatically. 'Yes.'

The girl uttered a sigh of relief and sank back once more. Miguel got to his feet and moved a little way away. Lisa followed, 'You're not satisfied are you?' she said.

He stared down at the floor. 'No. Isabel was right; she is making no progress at all.'

'What does it mean?'

He drew a sharp breath and looking at her said, 'She will never have the baby alive.'

Lisa gripped hold of his arm. 'There must be something we can do,' she said.

'Yes there is,' he said briskly, 'if I can get her to the hospital in time. Will you help?'

'Anything. I'll do anything. Just tell me.'

'If we can get her to the hospital in time we may be lucky. I want you to travel with her and make sure she gets jostled as little as possible.' He went over to where Manuela was lying and spoke to her and Isabel in a low voice. Isabel hurried out of the cabin and Lisa went over and crouched by Manuela. She slipped her cardigan off and helped the girl into it saying brightly 'It won't be long now.'

Miguel went out of the cabin and returned a minute later saying, 'We are ready.' He wrapped Manuela securely in a blanket and lifted her frail body easily. Lisa followed them outside; a crowd had gathered around the Land-Rover including the young man Isabel had thrown out of the cabin. He was waiting anxiously, twisting his frayed straw hat between his fingers.

Miguel put Manuela gently down on the mattress that had been laid in the back of the truck and Lisa tucked another blanket around her. When Miguel climbed down again the distracted boy rushed up to him babbling as incoherently as before. Miguel slapped him heartily on the back saying 'Relax my friend. You will be a father before the day is out.'

Lisa fervently hoped he would be right and as the truck jerked into motion she leaned forward to protect Manuela as much as possible.

The journey into Alhaja de mar was a nightmare Lisa would not easily forget. Manuela's pains became stronger although they were not more frequent than before and Miguel drove with deliberate slowness so as to avoid as much movement as possible in the back.

Darkness had already fallen by the time they arrived at the hospital. Lisa climbed down from the back of the Land-Rover uncaring about her hair, lank from perspiration, and her dirt-streaked dress. Her back ached; she longed to relax but knew she could not until she knew Manuela was all right. She felt as though she was going to be sick — not from squeamishness but from anxiety for the girl. She realised this was not time to give in to her own feelings so summoning every ounce of will power she possessed she followed them up the steps. Manuela's well-being had become something personal.

When she reached the corridor there was no sign of either Miguel or Manuela but when she reached the little office he was coming out, already rolling up his sleeves.

'Is there anything I can do to help?' she asked.

His face relaxed for a moment. 'You have done enough. It won't be long now. Why not go inside and rest? Perhaps you would telephone Mary and tell her what is happening. They will be worried.'

She had completely forgotten the Bannermans and she went straight to the telephone as Miguel hurried off down the corridor. The operator at the exchange took an age to connect her but she was grateful at least for only having to say, 'Señor Bannerman *por favour*' to be understood. This evening was no time for her to struggle with the language as well as her own churning emotions.

After a terse conversation with Mary who promised to send Philip out to collect her, Lisa replaced the receiver and went back into the corridor. As it was not a conventional hospital it took her quite some time to find the operating theatre and then she waited impatiently for what seemed like an age. The door was stout like all the doors in the old convent and no sound filtered through to the corridor.

Eventually she tensed as the door opened and two sisters looking incongruous in white theatre gowns wheeled Manuela out on a trolley. Lisa stared down at the still white face and back to the impassive faces of the sisters. There was nothing to tell her whether to be glad or not. They wheeled Manuela down the corridor and a minute later the door opened and Miguel came out, still wearing a theatre gown.

'She will be all right now,' he said, before Lisa could ask.

'And the child?'

He turned slightly to allow another sister to come out and she was carrying a tiny swaddled bundle. 'He is small but strong,' he said and Lisa went weak with relief, her eyes filling with tears. As the sister smilingly took the baby to join his mother she hardly heard him say under his breath in Spanish, 'Tomorrow there will be a better life for him.'

She looked at him questioningly but he was staring over her shoulder, through the window overlooking the courtyard. 'Philip is here. You have some good news to tell him.'

Lisa hesitated, unwilling to leave, despite her tiredness, and then she said, 'I'll go now. I'm glad everything worked out well.'

He had already started to move away but he turned and smiled briefly as he replied, 'So am I.'

Lisa ran down the corridor without looking back, and down the steps to the courtyard to meet Philip.

He greeted the news with relief. As he swung the station wagon around he said, 'We've been able to do nothing with Maria since Mary came back and told her. They have such huge families you'd think one child more or less wouldn't matter but you'd be surprised how devoted to each other they are.' He glanced across at her in the darkness as they sped back on the road to the plantation. 'You must be all in.'

'I was,' she admitted, 'but now I feel marvellous.'

Philip frowned but Lisa was too wrapped up in her own thoughts to notice but he caught her attention when he said, rather thoughtfully, 'Well don't let your emotions carry you away.' Her brow creased in perplexity as she waited for him to continue. 'What I mean is,' he went on with obvious difficulty, 'this kind of thing is all in a day's work to

Miguel but to you it's a drama you've never witnessed before.'

Her hands clenched in her lap and she thought. 'Does it show that much?' but said, 'I was just relieved for Manuela and her family. They were all so worried.'

'All the same I thought a word of warning wouldn't go amiss.' He paused for a moment and then said, 'As long as you realise he's not for you.'

'I know,' she replied firmly and was glad to complete the rest of the journey in silence. She knew Miguel belonged to Inés; that had been obvious from the start but Philip's reminder stung sharply; it made Philip seem so ambitious for a man he looked upon as a son in the absence of one of his own. Lisa needed no-one to tell her they were a well-matched pair and once married to Inés he would have no difficulty in getting all the new equipment he needed — and no doubt even a new hospital.

8

'I hope you haven't forgotten Christmas,' Mary said one morning.

Lisa looked up from the floor where she was cutting out cardboard furniture for the doll's house Philip had made for Rowena's birthday. 'I had. How can I even think about Christmas when the sun shines from morning till night and I wear nothing thicker than a cotton dress?'

'Well I was exactly the same when I first came out but the reason I reminded you was in case you wanted to send presents back to England. You'll need to send them soon if you want them to arrive in time.'

Lisa brushed her hair back with one hand, stood a little cardboard chair on the floor and got to her feet. She brushed off her dress and said, 'Next time Philip goes into town I shall go with him. One of those little shops in Calle Norte sells beautiful hand embroidered handkerchiefs and very cheaply too. As it's my first Christmas here I should be able to find some original gifts.'

'Philip is going in this afternoon if you're interested. And while you're there be a dear and post my parcels for me. You know how I hate going to town if I can help it. Philip has to go down to the harbour to arrange storing and shipping the sugar with the agent. We start harvesting right after Christmas.' She paused and then said casually, in a way that indicated Philip had told her of his warning. 'By the way Manuela came home yesterday.'

Lisa looked at Rowena who at that moment was preferable to Mary and replied, 'Good. I shall call in to see her.' She looked back to Mary, smiling brightly, 'Don't forget to give me your parcels and a list of anything else you need. I'll go and get ready now so I won't keep Philip waiting when he wants to set off.'

Rowena glanced up from her dolls. 'May I come with you?'

Lisa looked at her reprovingly. 'No. You have to read at least one chapter of your book and do all those sums I set you. You promised you'd do them this afternoon remember? When I agreed to make your furniture for you this morning.'

'Oh all right,' the little girl said grudgingly.

★　★　★

Lisa soon found all the presents she needed. She also bought a capacious straw bag to carry them in. When she had finished she found she still had plenty of time before she was to meet Philip so, inevitably, she wandered up the hill towards la plaza past the shabby hotels and cantinas. Beggars lurked in every doorway and in one a young man played a mournful tune on a guitar. In Alhaja everyone walked in the road and

Lisa was no exception. Frequently she was forced back onto the rubbish-strewn pavement by the insistent blaring of a motor horn; the car would then sweep past her still sounding its horn to warn other pedestrians. Most of the vehicles on the island seemed to be rattly contraptions held together by nothing stronger than good luck; others were plush American limousines like the president's and she knew they belonged to the wealthier plantation owners or the Americans living in the self-contained world of the oil refinery.

Once she reached la plaza her eyes were drawn towards the red roof of the hospital and then back to La Casa des flores. She contemplated visiting Inés but was reluctant to risk bumping into Señor Pantero or Luis Baldera.

She slipped a fine scarf over her head and pushing her arms into the sleeves of her cardigan she walked purposefully across the square to the once magnificent Church of Santa Angelina. There was still much of the former magnificence left inside the church, with its high vaulted ceiling and delicately chased stonework depicting scenes from the Passion. When she strolled back into the mid-afternoon sunshine she was more relaxed than she had been for some weeks; the tranquility of the church had had its effect on her.

One of the shaky old buses that linked the villages and towns of Santa Angelina with Alhaja de mar was pulling into the square and Lisa watched smilingly as it disgorged its load of passengers accompanied by an assortment of animals. The bus pulled away and she saw there was still a crowd by the wall. They were all laughing and cheering loudly. Just as she went forward to see what was happening someone pulled her back by the arm. She wheeled around sharply but Miguel was not looking at her, he was watching the crowd.

'Do you know what they are doing?' he asked.

'It looks as though somebody is painting that wall,' she explained.

A loud cheer rose from the crowd and Lisa could plainly see what the boy had painted in large red letters on the wall — 'Down with Pantero. Long live El Salvador.'

Miguel swore under his breath, muttering, 'The fool!'

He started forward just as the crowd suddenly melted away leaving the boy looking cowed, exposed for all to see. It was obvious a moment later what had caused the crowd to disperse — two jeeps were rolling down the hill from el alcazar towards the square.

Miguel stopped and turned back to Lisa. 'It is too late.' He gripped her arm and began to pull her away.

Stubbornly standing her ground she asked, 'What will happen to him?'

'He will be arrested of course.'

Lisa went rigid. 'You can't let them arrest him for that. It's only youthful bravado.' She glanced round and saw the soldiers jump out of the jeeps and push the boy against the wall and search him for weapons.

'Come along Lisa. You can't help.' He took her arm once more and led her away.

'But if they take him . . . oh we can't let them! He's committed no crime.'

'In Santa Angelina he has,' Miguel explained simply as the boy's hands were roughly tied behind his back.

Lisa pulled away from his restraining grip. 'I must do something. I shall go and speak to Señor Pantero. He'll listen to me. He's not an unreasonable man when you know him. You should speak to him but you won't! That boy won't mean a thing to you until they carry his broken body into the hospital!'

She began to run heedlessly across the square but she didn't get very far. A few strides and he caught up with her, forcibly pulling her back against a wall. 'You little idiot! Do you want them to take you too?'

'They can't,' she said defiantly. 'I have a British passport,' she told him, struggling fiercely against his iron grip.

As the soldiers piled back into the jeeps, this time with their prisoner, Miguel pushed her into a doorway. His face was very close to hers. 'A passport won't help you. There is no British consulate in Santa Angelina and by the time they secure your release some very nasty things could have happened to you.'

The jeeps were starting up. She gave him a malicious look and tried to get past him. 'You're always talking about the people and how you feel for them. Now I know it's all talk. There were times when I almost believed you cared — when you weren't so frightened of offending Pantero.'

His face tightened angrily and she saw with satisfaction her taunt had hit home. With a smile of triumph she made to pass him. 'I at least will try to *do* something.'

He pinned both her shoulders to the

door with his hands. 'You will go nowhere,' he said roughly. Before she could avoid it his lips were crushing down on hers — a kiss not to show love but to silence her until the danger had passed.

She struggled helplessly but his hands pinned her like a butterfly to a board and her frenzied pummeling had no effect. As she twisted her face away he relentlessly sought her lips with his own. She bit his lip as hard as she could. Her eyes glittered with defiance and anger as he pulled away sharply, snatching hold of her wrist in a cruelly tight grip.

'You little wildcat. How I should like to tame you.'

'Let me go,' she said through her teeth.

With one hand still gripping her wrist he pulled out his handkerchief and dabbed at his lips where she had drawn blood, each staring defiantly at the other. He did not lessen his hold on her while he stepped back into the street.

'They have gone.' He pulled her out in time for her to see the last jeep disappearing over the brow of the hill.

He let go of her at last. She wheeled around on him furiously. 'I hope you're satisfied with what you've done.'

He pushed his handkerchief back into his pocket. 'We could do nothing except land ourselves in trouble. You have no notion of how much trouble.'

'All I know is pretending injustice does not exist doesn't make it go away. That's how tyrants are made.'

His anger had evaporated and he said quietly. 'In future when you see an incident like that you will say and do nothing. Promise me.'

'I certainly will not promise. I have a conscience if you haven't.' She began to walk away only to be pulled back once more, but more gently this time.

'My conscience would prick if anything happened to you. I cannot let you go without your promise.'

Unwillingly she met his eyes. She couldn't admit he was right, although she knew he was. Now the heat of the moment had passed she was aware there was nothing she could have done to help the unfortunate victim.

'I promise,' she said at last.

He picked up her straw bag, forgotten in the doorway just as it had fallen and he handed it back. 'How are you getting back to the plantation?'

'I'm meeting Philip.' She glanced at her watch and gave a nervous laugh, 'Now.'

'Tell him I was asking after him. I shall be along to the plantation this week.'

'I'll tell him.' Suddenly she was shy. 'And thank you,' she said hesitantly, 'thank you for stopping me. It was an idiot thing to do. You can't win a war single handed.'

He studied her gravely for a while and then said lightly, 'Just don't let it happen again. I may not be around next time and believe me when I say it can be very rough up there for a woman.'

She walked slowly towards the road

to the harbour. When she reached the corner she paused to look back and he was still staring after her.

★ ★ ★

Lisa stood on the veranda of the bungalow watching the cloud of dust heralding the approach of a vehicle. She knew it was Miguel before she recognised the dusty Land-Rover. She had been expecting him to come, as he had promised — to see Philip. It had been three days since the incident in la plaza and since then they had heard the news that the boy who had been arrested was dead. Rumour had it he had fallen down a steep flight of stone steps in el alcazar in an attempt to escape. Even if the story were true to Liza it was a cruel waste of a life for the 'crime' of painting a slogan on a wall. A crime that would earn, at most, a rebuke from a British policeman.

During those three days she had often relived Miguel's kiss despite the knowledge that it had been a convenient way of silencing her when a hand over her mouth might have attracted unwelcome attention. A man and a woman kissing in a doorway was not an unusual sight in Alhaja de mar, but at the same time she repeatedly recalled the feel of his lips on hers and she couldn't help but wonder if he kissed Inés that way too. She knew, in her heart, he would not. Beneath a cool dedicated exterior she had glimpsed enough to tell her he possessed his share of the legendary Latin passion and for that one second when she succumbed to him she had been alarmed at the strength of her own ardour.

The only defence she had against her own inward turbulence was outward calm. Mentally she prepared herself to meet him as she watched the Land-Rover pull up in front of the bungalow. When he got out she made no move to go to meet him. His face she noticed was drawn with fatigue. It was not until he was climbing the veranda steps that he noticed her for the first time.

He stopped and she said coldly, 'Philip and Mary are out.'

He didn't answer straight away but came on to the veranda, 'You did not go with them?'

She looked away to the pile of parcels on the table behind her. 'I wanted to pack their Christmas presents and I'm not well acquainted with the people they're visiting. Would you like tea?'

He shook his head and she was uncomfortably aware of his continuous study of her. 'You heard about the boy?' he asked abruptly.

She turned away from him, 'Yes,' and began to gather up the paper and parcels from the table. She piled them into her unsteady arms and before she could protest he had taken them from her. He followed her inside and she said casually, 'Put them anywhere.'

He dropped them unceremoniously onto the sofa. 'I want to talk to you Lisa.'

She still did not look at him. 'Talk away,' she said with false brightness.

'No. Not here. Come with me somewhere more private.'

Involuntarily she moved a step further away and impatiently he added, 'There is nothing to fear. I assure you I will not force my attentions on you.'

Viciously she screwed some pieces of paper into a tiny ball and threw them into a paper basket. 'If you want to apologise for that you can take it you're forgiven.'

He took hold of her arm and she turned her startled gaze on him as he said harshly, 'I would not insult you by apologising.' He let her go and shaken by the suppressed emotion in his voice she sank down in a chair. He said in a more normal way, 'There are some things you should know. You should have been told when you arrived but no-one expected you to stay this long or,' he paused, 'to be the person you are.'

He turned and walked out of the

bungalow. Lisa, consumed with curiosity, followed. He waited in silence while she climbed in beside him. When they reached the main road he turned in the direction of the village instead of Alhaja de mar as she had expected him to do. Well before they reached the village he turned off the road into a clump of palm trees bordering a small, deserted beach.

'We will walk along the beach,' he said tersely and wordlessly she followed. When they reached another clump of palms he stopped, 'Shall we sit down?'

Had it been any other man but Miguel she would have suspected him of guile in getting her down here alone, but this *was* Miguel and she was convinced he would not waste his precious time unless it was for something important.

She could not draw her eyes away from his face as he stared out across the sand at a ship steaming across the line of the horizon. Then he looked at her.

'It is a big responsibility what I am about to tell you. I only hope I am right. It is about your father.'

Eagerly she leaned towards him. 'Yes?'

'We were friends, your father and I. He spoke often about you but even so when you came you were not what I expected.'

She looked away. 'I know what you expected — a girl out for a gay time. Perhaps you weren't so far wrong. I didn't expect Santa Angelina to be quite like it is.' She looked at him again. 'But that isn't what you want to tell me is it?'

'No.' He took a deep breath. 'Pantero told you your father was killed by the rebels during an ambush . . . ' Her heart momentarily constricted with rememberance of a pain she thought she had successfully buried deep inside her. He continued, 'He lied to you.' Before she could say anything he went on, quickly this time, 'Your father was killed because he was helping the rebel army.'

She pulled away as if stung. 'I don't believe you!'

'It is true Lisa. I swear to you it is true.'

She stared at him for a long time before asking woodenly. 'How did he die?'

'He was arrested and he was shot trying to escape from el alcazar.'

She closed her eyes in the vain hope that when she opened them again she would be back at the bungalow and all this would have been a nasty dream. But when she did open them she was still on the beach and Miguel was just a blurred image by her side. She shook her head in disbelief.

'He was with Pantero's army. My father would never be a traitor.'

'He was no traitor. During his service he came to love Santa Angelina and hate Pantero's subjection of his people. If there had been no rebel army he would have finished his term of service and gone on elsewhere, but a rebel army had been formed and he came into contact with . . . people connected with them. All they had was the will to fight so your father, in his off-duty time, trained them in the art of fighting. Those he trained trained others and so on. That is why they are so efficient today.'

'You knew all this?'

'Yes I knew.'

'And yet you didn't tell Pantero.'

'He was my friend. How could I tell on him?'

'But if you had you would have been a hero. From what you say the rebel's successes must be due to my father's training. You might even have been rewarded with a new hospital. Now you're in danger just for knowing.'

He smiled sadly. 'I know you think me heartless, but it is so. Besides I am quite safe. You must have realised I am in favour with el presidente.'

She knew he meant Inés. 'Why are you telling me this now?' she asked in a dull voice.

211

He hesitated a moment. 'Because some of the things you say, and do, could be misconstrued as unpatriotic. The government is very sensitive when it comes to loyalty — as it is entitled to be with the position as it is — and I should hate you to get into trouble. It would be so easy with your attitude.'

She met his gaze. 'Is compassion a crime too?'

He smiled. 'Of course not. But in view of your father's behaviour before his death it would be best if you kept your opinions to yourself. I know it is not easy for you to keep quiet when you see injustice but you cannot do anything so it is best not to try.'

She drew circles in the sand with her finger. 'I should be able to understand why my father risked and gave his life for them,' she said after a short silence, 'but I don't.'

'You have seen how poor people are here. This island has never left the nineteenth century and it has to if it and its people are to become prosperous. Under Pantero and his ruthless suppression of straight-forward opposition this can never be.'

The first shock that had stunned her was over and she was able to reason once more. 'What makes you think some idealistic fool in the hills is going to do anything more than waste more lives, even if he does manage to depose Pantero. Will the island become prosperous overnight? I doubt it.'

'If changes were started today we would not see the full benefit of them in our lifetime Lisa. Your mistake is in believing Santa Angelina is a poor country. It is the people who are poor, except for a few plantation owners.'

'It's the same thing.'

'No it is not,' he said gently. 'There are many natural resources that are not exploited to the full for the want of financial help. Sugar you already know. But there are also bananas, pineapples, coconuts. There is oil already mined inland and perhaps there is more in other areas. The hills are thick with mahogany, cedar and pine. And there is the biggest money maker of them all — tourism.'

'All very easily said Miguel. But Pantero is no fool. Why doesn't he exploit it?'

'He is no fool for his own pocket. For every bag of sugar exported, every carton of bananas, the growers pay a heavy tax to the state. Pantero says — and no one can dispute it — the money must pay for his army and their equipment.' He shrugged. 'So no new schools, hospitals or houses. No fat salaries to tempt teachers and doctors to come here.

'Several years ago, when I first came back to Santa Angelina, an American corporation approached Pantero with a view to building a hotel on one of the beaches. They considered Santa Angelina, with its good climate and absence of malaria, an attractive proposition for tourists who are always eager to sample somewhere new. They would find the poverty picturesque,' he smiled wryly, 'as long as they didn't have to stay at the hotels we have to offer.'

'What happened?'

Miguel turned to her and she was shocked at the disgust she read in his face. 'He asked an astronomical amount of money for the right to build and of course the Americans turned it down. When the tourists tire of the Bahamas and Jamaica, Pantero said, they would turn to Santa Angelina and then the Americans will pay even more for the right to build hotels and amenities. So again no hotel and gone was the chance of employment for hundreds of people. Pantero can afford to wait — Santa Angelina can't.'

Lisa said nothing and he went on, 'Pantero's forefathers were conquistadors just as mine were. They came to the Carribean to plunder the islands and exploit the people. It is still being done. Pantero will not allow the country to be opened up to foreign investment because he fears world opinion and he fears having his stranglehold on the people broken. He has been tolerated so long only because the majority of the islanders are ignorant and know nothing else. They have never lived in a free and prosperous country. I know my own sense of amazement when I first arrived in the United States when I was a boy and saw their standard of living. You are beginning to understand?'

Her eyes were fixed on his face. 'Yes I understand very well now. What I don't understand is why everyone lied to me.'

'When it happened everyone knew you were on your way here. The most obvious thing to have done was to hold you in custody for a while or to send you straight back. I was at La Casa des flores when Baldera brought the news of your father's death. After Pantero had finished raging Baldera suggested suppressing the story — few people knew your father was helping the rebels and if anyone admitted knowing about his death they also accused themselves of being implicated with the rebels. Suppressing news is a simple matter here. Baldera gave the president the idea that you might know something of your father's activities and could be useful.'

'That's why my letters were stolen. But there was nothing in them.'

'Your father was too much of a professional to write to you about what he was doing. He knew letters were often intercepted. They also wondered if you had been given the job of raising funds in Britain for the rebels. We were all instructed to regard your father as a hero of the republic and treat you accordingly with respect. If you knew about your father's secret activities and you were given to understand they didn't it was hoped you would try and contact the rebels.'

'But I didn't.'

'No they realised that you were innocent but it didn't stop them hoping someone would contact you.'

'So that was why he wanted me to stay and why Luis was so attentive.'

He smiled kindly. 'Yes. I am sorry.'

She smiled back. 'So am I. I understand now why you were so hostile to me when I first arrived. I suppose you resented my acceptance of hospitality from the man who killed my father.'

'No,' he said gently, 'you couldn't know about that. Luis and Inés had to be more than friendly to you but I thought it would be better if I was more like a loyal Santa Angelinan, despising you for being your father's daughter, while obeying my president by being polite. It worried me when I saw you were becoming disposed towards the under-dog.'

Lisa traced another few circles in the sand. 'Inés knew too.'

'Don't judge her too harshly Lisa. She obeyed her father because she is afraid of him. She was very reluctant to agree; she is an unwilling tool.' Lisa remembered the conversation in the

218

salon she had overheard and knew it to be true. 'The note Paco gave you in the square was from her. It was her way of warning you. I questioned him the same day and he told me who had paid him to deliver it.' He paused and she sensed his eyes on her averted face. 'You should pity her Lisa. She is torn between loyalty to her father and what she knows to be right.'

Her chin quivered slightly. 'You said my father was arrested and taken up to el alcazar . . . '

'They did not harm him. He tried to escape first. He was a brave man but he dared not risk betraying his friends.'

The tears she had contained for so long began to flow silently down her cheeks. Suddenly, able to bear it no longer, she scrambled to her feet and began to run blindly along the beach until she came to the spindly trunk of a palm tree. She clung onto it, her body racked with convulsive sobs.

The soft powdery sand cloaked the sound of his approaching footsteps and

Lisa was unaware of his presence until he took her into his arms. She stayed there for what seemed to be an age, sobbing unashamedly. When it ceased at last he gave her his handkerchief to dry her eyes and the sight of it, bloodstained from the time she had bit him almost started her crying again. He always appeared to be so self-sufficient but he was incapable of providing himself with so much as a clean handkerchief.

'I always regarded him as a hardened soldier and a very selfish man,' she said, taking a deep breath. 'I didn't really know him until today.'

'Perhaps he was both but at least he had feelings. He knew there would, one day, be fighting on this island and he did not want it to be a senseless one way slaughter. He knew he was playing a very dangerous game and I think he sensed he would never leave Santa Angelina alive. That was why he wanted to see you again. He too realised you were strangers to each other and while he could he wanted to amend that, although I warned him of the possible danger to you and tried to persuade him to leave you in England.'

She looked at him levelly. 'Now you've told me all this you too are in danger.'

He glanced around. 'There is no one to overhear us and,' he smiled suddenly, 'I do not think you will tell on me.'

At last she was able to smile back. 'I'm very grateful to you Miguel. Do the Bannermans know?'

'Yes. They too thought it best for you not to have the strain of pretending. That was why they had you come to the plantation. It is dangerous for them too as you will realise. While your father was supposed to be at their bungalow he was with the rebels.'

'I don't know what to say. You've all risked so much for my father and myself.'

His face was in shadow; she could not read the expression in his dark eyes but it was instinct that drew them together and a moment later she was back in his arms. When his lips met hers there was no struggle to escape. Her nails bit into the thin material of his jacket as his kiss scorched her lips and stirred in her a spark that would never be extinguished as long as she lived.

Her head told her he belonged to another but it was her heart that knew he was hers for this one moment of rapture and she would relive that moment for ever more. They were alone on the beach; the sun smiled benignly above them, the sea caressed the shore with a sigh and they were the only people in the world.

'If only I could have met you sooner,' he whispered into her ear and, releasing her abruptly he turned and walked back along the beach.

She remained by the tree staring after him helplessly before she began to run. 'Wait!' she shouted as she caught up with him.

He stopped and looked at her dispassionately. 'It is too late. My heart is no longer mine to give you. I must take you back. Mary and Philip will be worried if they come home and find you gone.'

She smiled reassuringly despite the storm raging inside her. 'A minute more won't make any difference. You don't have to feel badly Miguel. I don't know what the conventions are in Santa Angelina but in England there is no shame in two people who are attracted kissing each other.' He watched her intently as she spoke and she continued, saying softly, 'I know how things are with you and Inés and I promise I'll never embarrass either of you over today.'

He shook his head slowly in disbelief. 'Inés has nothing to do with this. I only wish it were so simple. Another woman would never keep me away from you.' As if suddenly aware of saying too much he turned and hurried back to the Land-Rover, leaving Lisa once more astounded and confused.

A second later she started to go after

him but her feet could get little purchase on the slippery sand and she had to struggle desperately in her haste to reach him. When she clambered into the Land-Rover he was already hunched over the wheel staring out to sea.

'Don't you think you owe me an explanation?' she said, a little breathlessly.

He still did not look at her. 'No, although I *can* give you some advice — go back to England, settle down and forget you ever knew me.'

'Just like that,' she whispered to herself.

He started up the engine. She looked at him. 'I love you,' she said softly. 'If you tell me it's hopeless I'll accept it but at least let me know why.'

He switched off the engine. 'I can't. For your own sake I can't.'

'It's something to do with my father isn't it?'

He turned to face her then. 'I will tell you this Lisa, Pantero will soon be challenged for the leadership of this country. He will not step down and there will be civil war. War is never pleasant but civil war is even worse. I will not risk you involved in that.'

She looked directly into his eyes, now soft and warm. 'I've made Santa Angelina my home. I'm not afraid of being caught up in its troubles. I won't be the only woman involved.'

'But you are the only woman I care about.'

She took his hand in hers. 'We'll be safe Miguel. You will be in the hospital and both sides will respect it as neutral territory.'

He pulled his hand away and banged his clenched fist down on the steering wheel. 'That is just it Lisa. I will not be at the hospital. I will be with the rebels.'

She stared at him in disbelief for a moment and then said quickly, breathlessly, words tumbling incoherently on one another, 'Well, I realised you were in sympathy with them to a certain degree but there's no need for false heroics. As a doctor you'll be needed at the hospital. I can understand your desire to help but the best way you . . . '

'Stop Lisa! Please stop!' Then he said softly. 'Our people, thanks to your father, have the ability to fight. They are courageous. That is why Baldera has never succeeded in making any of them talk. They regard themselves unimportant — expendable. The only thing that is important is the future for their children. A future free and prosperous. They will fight but they have to be led by those better able to do it. Most of them cannot even read or write. How can they follow maps and written orders?'

Suddenly she was angry. 'So you're going to fight. And what will happen to all the injured who will be brought to the hospital while you're out injuring and killing more?'

'Dr. Lim is more than capable. The sisters are all well trained and in addition the Americans have provided a doctor and several nurses for the staff at the oil refinery and they will certainly help. Pantero as the legitimate head of government will be able to call in all the help he needs from the outside. The rebels will have casualties too and who will help them? If I stayed at the hospital do you imagine I would be allowed to aid any of their injured? No, Lisa I am committed.'

Her eyes were steely hard. 'By my father?'

He met her gaze steadily, 'No, it was I who committed him.'

The only sound that could be heard was the gentle whisper of the surf meeting the shore. 'You've been with them all the time,' she said incredulously. He looked away and she said, 'It makes no difference to the way I feel about you Miguel.'

His eyes full of love and warmth were drawn back to hers. 'Go back to England *querida*. When this is all over I will come for you.'

'You're very sure of winning aren't you?'

'We have to. It is the only chance we have of having a country worth living in. Did you know Philip is the only plantation owner who gives his workers decent living accommodation and pays them a reasonble wage? Pantero only cares about receiving his taxes and if they are paid, all is well.'

'You know I won't go away Miguel. Do you really think my feelings for you are so shallow?'

'You have no choice. Once civil war breaks out Pantero will panic and arrest all those even remotely connected with known sympathisers. I can look after myself but I am not willing to risk that for you.'

Suddenly her control broke at the sound of the love and concern in his voice. 'Oh don't send me away Miguel! Please don't send me away. If there is one thing my parent's marriage taught me it's that a woman must accept her man for what he is. My parents shared nothing. They must have loved each other at the beginning but because they took the safest way they lost it all. There's no-one else in the world I can love after you. Do you want me to spend the rest of my life wondering where you are, if you're alive or dead?' Her voice took on a pleading note. 'I don't care if we have one week or a lifetime together; all I ask is that we share it together.'

The golden ball of light was sinking in a flaming sky as he gathered her into his arms saying, 'Heaven knows I need you more than ever now.'

9

Lisa drew a deep sigh of contentment as she gazed out at the sea. She felt she could never tire of the view from the Bannerman's beach bungalow.

Almost a year had passed; another sugar crop, another rainy season and soon another Christmas.

The village school had become a reality. Not only were most of the children reading and writing but also those young mothers unable to work in the fields; they too insisted on joining the classes. Manuela, bringing her baby along, proved to be the most apt pupil and she was now an invaluable assistant to Lisa whenever she got into difficulties with the language.

There had been clouds on the horizon too, when there had been news of raids or ambushes by the rebels, now becoming more frequent, and when

Miguel went into the hills or the country — ostensibly for a professional visit to the villages. He never enlightened her if he was doing otherwise but if a raid occurred when he was away she fretted until he returned. Each week there were fresh rumours of revolution but as everything was outwardly calm Lisa deluded herself it would never happen.

Her hardest task was facing Señor Pantero or Inés and pretending to be loyal to them. Miguel did it marvellously, even giving the president advice on how to deal with the rumoured rebellion. She hated the subterfuge but knew it was all too necessary — their lives depended on it.

She slipped off her sandals and ran down the steps, her toes sinking into the sand. She could see him lying beneath the shade of a coconut palm, face down, his head resting on his arms.

Silently she ran across the beach and for a moment stared down at him as he lay there unaware of her presence. With a mischievous smile on her face she stooped down to fill her hand with sand, allowing it to filter through her fingers onto his sun-bronzed back.

There was no response but when she stooped to gather another handful he turned and pulled her down beside him kissing her as she struggled beneath him.

'You cheat!' she cried. 'I thought you were asleep.'

'I was but I always know when you are missing. I saw you running across the sand. Where have you been?'

'Preparing our dinner of course.' She sat up, hugging her knees. 'I've sent Lucia back to the village. While we're here I want to do everything myself.'

He sank back on to the sand with his arms behind his head, watching her. 'I hope it is worth the effort and the amount of time you were absent from my side.'

'Lucia brought some fresh mackerel this morning and I've made coconut cream for our bananas. And to start the whole thing off avocado pear and freshly caught prawns. Lucia can vouch for the fish; it's from her father's boat. You wouldn't get a better meal at the Savoy in London.'

'I'd much rather have it here with you.'

Their eyes met in a moment of mutual understanding and then she rolled over and lay down next to him, her face close to his. She sifted sand through her fingers thoughtfully. 'Do you realise if I'd gone back to England like you asked me to we would have missed this year?'

He sat up. 'Is it really a year?'

She nodded gravely. 'Next month is our anniversary. One whole year of marriage.'

'You were right *querida*.'

She rolled over again and looked up at him diffidently. 'Don't you think it merits a kiss?'

He bent over her and brushed her lips with his own and with a laugh she pulled him down beside her again. She settled her head on his chest, gazing up at the infinitous sky filled with swooping gulls.

'Inés took it well didn't she?'

'Our marriage you mean?'

'What else? I had visions of her clawing my eyes out. I could hardly blame her, could I?'

He laughed. 'Inés will never want for the attention of a man.'

'She was in love with you, and very sensibly too.'

'Perhaps a little.'

'And you? Didn't you find her very beautiful?'

'I was a little attracted for a while I suppose — until I saw you. There was never any question of anything more than a pleasant friendship. I am ashamed to say I used her company to stay close to the president. Luckily he regarded my presence on the island as rather a feather in his cap because I left the United States to come here.' He ran his fingers through her silky hair. 'It hardly matters now.'

'There's not even a breeze today,' she said with a sigh. 'I could stay here forever.'

'Me too.' He paused and then said, 'You know nothing has changed Lisa?'

'Yes, I know. I never look beyond tomorrow.'

'There are times when all I want to do is take you and get on the first boat out of here.'

'There is nothing to stop you Miguel,' she said in a level voice.

'But there is *querida*. You know I cannot leave here now. The revolution will go ahead and if we lose I would always blame myself for the failure. If we lose and I am here I will, at least, know I had done my best.'

Lisa's heart was heavy when she added to herself; if you're alive to know. When she spoke her voice was thick, 'You're only one man Miguel. If you're . . . if anything should happen to you what would they do?'

'There are others of course. I am only one among many.'

235

'Exactly. So you *are* dispensable?'

He laughed. 'You are very persuasive. If I had met you before I became involved nothing could have made me join them. But now I am committed.'

'Do I know any of the others?'

'Yes, but I shall not tell you who they are, so please don't ask.'

She hesitated a moment and then said, 'So you must know the man they call El Salvador.'

He hesitated too and then said tersely. 'Yes.'

She rolled over to face him. 'I won't ask you who he is but tell me one thing if you know and then I can be a little easier in my mind . . . '

'I shall try to answer.'

'Does he really care about improving conditions in the country or is he just trading on highly charged emotions in order to gain power for its own sake? It's happened so many times before in history Miguel. If he's that kind of man he'll be no better than Pantero — perhaps a good deal worse — and I can't bear to think my father might have died uselessly or you're risking your life to further one man's greedy ambition.'

'He is sincere Lisa. I promise you he is sincere.'

'Are you really sure Miguel?'

'Yes I am sure.'

She laid her head down on his chest once more and stared up at the sky. 'What will happen when you've won?'

'The new regime will build schools, hospitals and so on. Make education compulsory, fix a minimum wage for the plantation workers. There is so much to do. When other countries see what we are trying to do we will have no difficulty in obtaining loans.'

'I wish it was all over Miguel and then we could settle down and live our lives without having to look over our shoulders all the time.'

His arm came around her. 'We must be patient. We may go on like this for years — fighting where we can, harrassing the government and gaining support until the time to overthrow Pantero comes. We have no other choice but to enjoy life while we can.'

She turned her face up to his. 'We'll make every minute count, won't we?'

'Yes *amor mio* we will,' he said and their lips met, blotting out the past and the future; all that mattered was the present.

*   *   *

Her eyes focused slowly and then she sat up sharply when she saw him closing the suitcase. 'Why are you up so early?'

He wheeled around at the sound of her voice and smiled sheepishly. 'I hoped you would be able to sleep a little longer. I tried not to disturb you.'

Her feet met the cool tiled floor as she slipped out of bed, panic rising swiftly within her breast. 'Something is wrong isn't it?'

He put a reassuring hand on her arm. 'There is no panic *querida*. There has been a hurricane warning and we must return to Alhaja immediately. Orlando has come to warn us and he will take us back in his boat.'

Her eyes were full of disbelief. 'Hurricane? But we're not in the hurricane belt.'

'Only just outside Lisa. A freak hurricane hit Alhaja a hundred years ago. There is always the possibility of it happening again. But do not be alarmed; very likely it will change course and miss the island completely.'

Lisa went across to the window and opening the shutters she saw a hazy sun had already risen. 'But it's so still Miguel. There's no sign of a storm.'

'The stillness itself is a bad sign.'

She turned and smiled apologetically. 'I won't be more than a few minutes getting dressed.'

'Good. I have already packed your clothes. I hope you like what I left out.'

She laughed. 'You're better than having a personal maid.'

The rickety fishing boat was waiting

by the pier surrounded by all the village fishing boats that, for once, had not put out to sea. Orlando was always the one to transport them to and from the bungalow but each time she had to board the boat Lisa always looked at it askance, convinced it would break up and sink long before their destination was reached.

When they reached the pier Lisa looked back at the bungalow now locked and deserted — and she wondered when they would be able to steal another few days together at the place she had come to love so much.

Miguel sensing her thoughts said gently, 'We will come again soon.' But sadly she knew the demands made on him would make it a long time before they returned to the little cove. He threw the case to Orlando, swinging Lisa into his arms and carrying her onto the boat.

The old man's wrinkled face broke into a wide grin and Lisa exchanged a few words with him before she settled down for the journey back. Around her lay Orlando's fishing nets and the all-pervading smell of fish.

After speaking to Orlando for a few moments Miguel came over and sat down beside her. The engine throbbed into life and the boat moved out into the bay.

'If it is a false alarm we will come back,' he said, as she gazed out at the horizon.

She turned to look at him. 'You know we won't.'

He smiled sadly. 'Life with me is terrible. I did warn you.'

She slipped her hand into his and said gruffly, 'It's wonderful and you know it.' She turned to stare out at the sea once more. 'Will it be very terrible Miguel?'

He put his arm around her shoulders and drew her nearer. 'We will be safe enough at the hospital. Most of the buildings in Alhaja are strong. They have been standing for many hundreds of years.'

'But what of the people who don't live in solid buildings?'

'They will know what to do,' he said simply.

By the time the boat had rounded the headland the sky was filled with dark clouds, a strong wind had sprung up and they were forced to go into the tiny cabin. The boat surged up and down in the foaming water. White capped waves dashed over the deck and over the cabin until it seemed as though the boat could not possibly stay afloat.

It was with profound relief that Lisa caught sight of the familiar harbour of Alhaja de mar. There were several inter-island schooners tied up against the wharf, their sails folded, giving them a weird and ghostly appearance.

They were drenched to the skin from the foam and rain, just climbing from the boat to the wharf. Orlando tied up his boat and shouting his good-bye made off in the opposite direction to join his family who had already gone to safety.

As Lisa and Miguel hurried in the enveloping darkness from the harbour towards the square they had to stop and shelter in doorways every so often to catch their breath before continuing to struggle up the hill again. The streets were unusually empty and the shutters on every building were firmly closed. Lisa clung on to Miguel as they wrestled with the ever increasing wind and rain. When they finally reached la plaza, a place normally bustling with activity, it was horribly deserted.

It took a long time for them to cross even the hospital courtyard so wild was the wind as it fought against their efforts and drowned out the rumble of thunder. At last they reached the steps and Miguel slammed the door, bolting it firmly.

Lisa sank back against the wall, exhausted from the effort of battling against the raging force of the wind. Her clothes clung wetly to her back, her hair was plastered to her face and water streamed down to form a pool at her feet.

'We made it,' she said with a laugh after she had caught her breath. He too was soaked and gasping, his hair curling damply round his head. 'What do we do now?'

'First of all we get out of these clothes,' he replied, wiping his face, 'or the sisters will have two more patients to care for. And then we must make preparations.' He glanced around. 'At least all the shutters have been fixed into place.' He turned his attention back to Lisa, reaching out for her. 'Come. There is much we have to do.'

Back in their tiny room Lisa soon felt much better once she had put on dry clothes. She wondered if Miguel would return to tell her how she could help; characteristically he had changed in remarkably quick time and had already gone to see what needed to be done.

She wandered back towards the hospital section, flinching as the shutters rattled in her ears. White overalled maids were hurrying everywhere, but there was no sign of Miguel.

Finally she found Dr. Lim issuing loud instructions to two of the sisters, their bearing in the face of such danger was as impassive as ever. Their ability to carry on unflaggingly — along with Miguel and the other doctor — was forever a source of amazement to her.

'Señora Rodriguez,' he said, bowing low, 'you enjoyed your holiday I trust.'

'Yes it was very nice. Have you seen my husband?'

'A few minutes ago. He was looking in on his own patients.' He shook his head sadly. 'These patients will be safe, it is those who come after the storm has died down who will need our help.'

Over his shoulder Lisa caught sight of Miguel hurrying towards her. 'Ah there you are,' he cried, 'Come with me.'

He took her hand and led her along the corridor to a room where the sisters were busy making bandages and splints. Lisa unhesitatingly joined in and for the next few hours, together with the silent sisters, she helped prepare for the aftermath of the hurricane raging outside the stout hospital walls. As on many occasions before she wished the sisters gossiped like other women instead of only speaking when absolutely necessary; she needed something to take her mind off the frightening roar of the wind and rain that even the walls of the old convent could not shut out. She couldn't stop her mind dwelling on all the flimsy shacks existing all over the island — the ones that could be felled by one blow of a strong wind.

Each time the velocity of the wind and rain rose to shrieking pitch Lisa had the rash urge to scream, but one glance at the tranquil faces of the sisters and she was ashamed of her own weakness.

When they finished at last and Lisa felt her fingers would fall off and her eyes could stay open no longer she helped serve the evening meal to the patients. Elsewhere in the hospital spare beds, mattresses and bed clothes were being turned out in preparation for the influx of casualties. Beds in all the wards were pushed closer together to make room for the extra ones. Throughout the endless day the sisters carried out their duties in a calm that earned Lisa's eternal admiration.

She hadn't seen Miguel since they snatched a quick cup of coffee in the late afternoon and he had left her afterwards to go and prepare the theatre as it would undoubtedly be needed.

Finally everything that could be done was finished. She was coming out of the children's ward when she saw him hurrying down the corridor towards her. Fatigue was etched quite clearly on his face — if everyone else was working hard she knew he would be doubly so.

'You must finish now,' he said, touching her cheek with his finger. 'You are tired.'

'We all are. You too.'

'There is nothing more we can do tonight. Every patient has been given a

247

sedative, so now it is our turn to rest.'

The wind shrieked and howled like something unearthly as it hurled bullets of demented rainwater against the shutters. Lisa went rigid with fear at the sound of a terrific crash outside. 'What was that?'

'Only a tree in the courtyard. Come along *querida* we need sleep.'

She only realised how tired she really was when they were walking back to their room, their arms entwined around each other. When they reached it Lisa suddenly realised the roar had abated and she turned joyously saying, 'Listen darling. It's stopping!'

'Only for a short while unfortunately. It will start again soon.'

Wearily she sat down in front of the mirror and began to remove the pins from her hair. She swept a brush through it with comforting strokes. 'Do we really have to go through it all again?'

'You will be asleep.' He handed her a glass of milky liquid. 'Drink this.'

She continued brushing her hair. 'I don't need anything to make me sleep. I've really been asleep for hours even though my eyes have been open.'

He put his hands on her shoulders and kissed the nape of her neck and her hair at the top of her head. 'If you do not drink it the noise outside will keep you awake. I shall take one too. There will be a great deal to do tomorrow but we need rest before we can tackle it.'

She looked up at him as he leaned over her. 'Kiss me first Miguel.'

He kissed her gently on the lips and she responded with a passion borne of desperation. 'Do not be afraid *amor mio* it will soon be over.'

She turned her face to the wall. 'I'm not afraid of the hurricane. This is the first one for a hundred years and I feel this one is a bad omen.'

He turned her face round so that she had to look at him. 'There are no bad omens for us Lisa,' he said softly, 'You will see.'

As the wind began to rise again,

dashing rain and stones like missiles against the shutters, tearing tiles from the roofs and dashing them in a thousand fragments on the cobbles below, Lisa could not halt the fear growing inside her; a fear that their year of perfection was drawing to a close.

She awoke to the sound of the shutters being drawn back. It was hardly light but Miguel was dressed. No screaming wind assaulted her ears.

'It's over,' she said with a sigh.

'Yes it is over. Now we must find out what damage has been done.'

Lisa hurried across to the window and stared in dismay at the destruction outside. Sheets of corrugated iron and wood lay amidst broken tiles and fallen trees. Those trees left standing were stripped of foliage and they leaned precariously in the direction of the wind where they had been made to do homage to the all-powerful hurricane.

The first trickle of casualties were already coming in and before long the trickle had swelled to become a flood.

Lisa was soon applying bandages, wheeling trolleys and filling syringes as though she had been doing it all her life. The burden thrust upon them was lightened a little by the first aid station that had been set up by the medical team from the oil refinery in one of the hotels on Calle Norte and only the most seriously injured were being sent to the hospital.

Lisa wanted to weep at the sight of the broken bodies being wheeled in and out continuously and had she not been worked so unceasingly she would have given in and done so. But there was not time for personal indulgencies.

President Pantero on a tour of the stricken island called in during the morning, mouthing platitudes and smiling benevolently at the patients, then escaping as quickly as he could.

The stream abated slightly late in the evening and the staff were able to snatch their first meal of the day, although except for the maids whose appetites were ever healthy no-one could eat very much through sheer fatigue.

Lisa watched Miguel anxiously when he returned from his final round of the newly admitted patients; he had had ten unbroken hours in the operating theatre and she knew he was worried over the imminent danger of running out of drugs.

All day news had drifted in of whole coastal villages being washed out to sea and metal roofs being torn off and borne along in the wake of the howling hurricane to wreak even more damage. Mercifully, although the whole island had suffered to some extent, it was only the immediate vicinity of Alhaja de mar that had been badly affected.

'You'll have to take a break Miguel,' she said reprovingly. 'You'll be less than useless otherwise.'

'I know. There is nothing more I can do until it is light again, so we can get some sleep for a few hours at least. As soon as it is light we are going out to see what needs to be done.'

'I'll come with you.'

'No, it is the work for trained hands. You will be more useful here. Some of the sisters will be coming with me and also the American team will be going out. And for once Pantero has put his army to good use, clearing debris and rescuing the injured.'

'Are things very bad out there?' she asked anxiously.

'Bad enough from what I hear. The danger now is from epidemics and we have no typhoid vaccine.' For a moment he tore his mind away from his problems and smiled down at her. 'I have involved you too much in our problems *querida*.'

'I would have been involved without you,' she said softly and added, 'but with nothing like the satisfaction.'

At first light he was up again and for the next three days Lisa only saw him in passing, when he returned to the hospital for fresh supplies of drugs and dressings. Everyone snatched sleep where they could and when they could. Victims with injuries that couldn't be treated on the spot were sent back to the already overflowing hospital and amazingly room was found for them. Each new patient brought his or her own story of the damage done by the hurricane; Lisa listened sympathetically, bathed them, dressed their minor wounds expertly, cooked meals and fed those unable to fed themselves, thus leaving the sisters free for the actual nursing. There came a time when she forgot she had worn the same clothes for three days and nights or even that she was in desperate need of a bath and sleep. In the midst of it all she thought, 'This is what it will be like if there is a revolution, only then I won't have the satisfaction of knowing Miguel is safe.'

The desperate flow of humanity slowed on the third day. When at last they were able to rest Lisa was the last to go, waiting anxiously for his return. Eventually, unable to keep her eyes open any longer, she threw herself into bed and fell into the deep sleep of exhaustion. When she awoke it was to find Miguel beside her, fast asleep. Her eyes were drawn to the clothes he had discarded and thrown in a heap on the floor — they were virtually unrecognisable, caked with mud and stained with dried blood. She sank back satisfied he had returned safely and went back to sleep.

'Are conditions very bad?' she asked the next morning as she watched him tuck into a hearty breakfast — his first proper meal since the hurricane struck.

'Not as bad as they might have been,' he replied vaguely. 'There was ample warning and many people went up into the high ground to safety. From what I hear the hurricane only struck the immediate district around Alhaja so the rest of the island escaped the main force of the wind. The shanty town has gone though.'

'Good job too,' she said. 'Now perhaps those people will get some proper accommodation.'

'I would not rely on that Lisa. They are already searching for driftwood to repair the shacks.'

'But what has happened to the people who lived there?'

He avoided her eyes. 'The worst casualties come from there but those who were able to have gone into the hills too.'

'The hills! But why Miguel?'

He pushed his plate away and studied her for a moment. 'When was the last time you had some fresh air?'

She looked perplexed. 'When we came back just before the hurricane. Why do you ask?'

He stood up and pulled her to her feet. 'You look pale. You need some air. Come along and we will walk for a while outside.'

Puzzled and a little afraid she allowed him to lead her outside to the courtyard that had been cleared of debris by soldiers under Pantero's orders. Miguel tucked her arm into his. 'I will tell you exactly what is happening,' he said. 'Today much of the responsibility for the welfare of the patients is being taken off our hands. The International Red Cross is flying in antibiotics, morphine and typhoid vaccine by helicopter this afternoon and also a team of doctors and nurses trained in disaster work . . . '

'But that's marvellous . . .'

'Hush, let me finish. As always my love we have little time. The worst part of all this is the number of families who are now homeless. There are thousands from the shanty town alone — that is where I have been these past days. But now I have learned supplies of blankets, tents and food are coming by sea and they should arrive in a day or two.'

'Thank goodness,' she breathed.

'Yes it is good news. Even Pantero could not refuse foreign aid on this occasion.'

She stopped walking, alarm darkening her eyes. 'Have you any news of Philip and Mary?'

He smiled. 'They are safe.' He laughed then. 'I don't know how they managed to do it but they squeezed everyone of their workers into the bungalow.' He became serious. 'But their crop is ruined as it is all over the island.'

'Oh no Miguel. What will happen?'

'There will be no harvest this year or next either. That is why the men have gone to the hills.' He stood and faced her, his hands gripping the upper part of her arms. 'They have nothing to lose now, that is why they want to join the rebel army.'

She stared at him woodenly, fear freezing her blood. Instinct told her the moment she had dreaded for the past year was about to come. Her voice when she spoke was harsh. 'What are you trying to tell me?'

'I have to go — only for a few days Lisa.'

'But what about the hospital? The patients?'

'I have done all I can. When the relief teams get here they will take over. There will no longer be the risk of epidemic and the island is already getting back to normal. Rafael has already left. Consuela and the children have gone to a safe place — just in case.'

Lisa stared at him increduously. 'Rafael? Not Rafael surely?'

He laughed at her amazement. 'Yes Rafael. He appears to be nothing more than an amiable buffoon — a playboy — but he has an excellent brain and he really cares.

'We must go and help organise those who wish to join us Lisa. The more we have the better chance of winning without a fight.'

'You'll be missed. They'll know where you've gone.'

'No. There is still much confusion. I will not be missed for a few days and if I am it will be thought I am still out looking for casualties. It is a good opportunity while the army is occupied with salvage and rescue operations.' He paused before saying pleadingly, 'I must go. These men must be trained if they are to be useful and training must be organised.'

Lisa managed to smile. 'I know Miguel.'

His face registered relief. 'I am a very lucky man to have a wife like you.' He turned back towards the steps and said more briskly, 'I am going to check around the wards and there are instructions to be left and while I am doing it you can pack the things you will need for the next few days. I shall take you to the plantation to wait for my return.'

Lisa stopped in her tracks. 'The plantation? But I want to stay here.'

'And I want you to stay with Philip,' he said patiently. 'If anything should happen to me he will take care of you — and there is much to do at the plantation too.'

She smiled resignedly. 'I'll be ready when you've finished your round.'

10

It was Lisa's first trip outside the hospital grounds since the hurricane had struck and although much of the debris had been cleared away she was still shocked at the amount of damage. In Alhaja every building had lost at least some of its tiles, balconies were hanging precariously off the walls and shutters swung off their hinges. As the road descended into the valley she could see countless numbers of trees uprooted completely and others, devoid of foliage, bent almost horizontal in the path of the wind.

There was still a pervading odour of decay in the air as they passed the ruined remains of the shanty town. The sound of banging filled the air as men, women and children joined in a common effort to repair the damage to their pitiful homes. The sides of the road were piled with rubbish, palm leaves, broken bits of furniture and corrugated sheets that once formed a roof over a family's head. The road swarmed with dust-stained and mud-splattered people who were eagerly sifting through the rubble hoping to salvage something they could use to rebuild their homes. And in a slowly moving file homeless families advanced towards Alhaja carrying the pitifully few belongings they had managed to save.

The road itself had been under water during the deluge and had been turned into a sea of mud. Now there were deep clefts where it had dried out and Lisa was jolted continuously during the journey. When they reached the cane fields she gasped at the sight of the once tall and stately blades of sugar cane, now lying broken and crushed on the ground.

Miguel smiled across at her, 'In two years you will not know there had been a hurricane.'

'I know, but until then . . . '

Lisa was relieved when she saw how little damage had been done to the bungalow itself. When Lisa went inside, followed by Miguel carrying her case, she couldn't help but laugh at the number of mattresses laid side by side on the floor.

'It was funnier still when everyone was sleeping here,' Mary said, coming out of her room carrying a pile of clean laundry.

'Where is all your furniture?' Lisa asked.

'We had to move it outside to make room for everyone and I'm afraid there was very little left when we went out to get it. Never mind,' she said briskly, 'It was better to know everyone was safe inside. The cabins weren't strong enough to shelter them against the wind. We were lucky — our roof stayed on, our generator is still working and we still have a good supply of water.' She paused. 'Come along in Lisa, you've had a rough few days.'

'Not as rough as the homeless and

injured,' she said with an expressive sigh. 'Has everyone gone back to the village now?'

'Most of them — all of the men. There wasn't as much damage as we feared and the damage that was done is being rapidly repaired. Philip is down at the village now. All we have to do now is get water down there and return all the mattresses. There are a couple of casualties down there too Miguel; will you look in before you go?'

'Of course Mary. I have to go down to collect any volunteers who want to come with me.'

Lisa and Miguel looked at each other and Mary said suddenly, 'Excuse me a moment will you? I want to get this laundry distributed; my kitchen is full of half naked women and children.'

When she had gone Lisa turned to Miguel again. 'When are you going?'

His eyes took in every detail of her features as if he were etching them indelibly on his memory. 'Now.'

'So soon?'

'The sooner I go the sooner I will be back.' He took her hand and studied it for a moment. 'Come outside with me Lisa.'

They walked onto the veranda, her hand in his. Her face was wet with tears as he took it in his hands. He stooped and kissed her lightly on the lips before turning wordlessly and walking over to the Land-Rover. Silent tears streamed down her face as she watched him drive away without a backward glance.

'*Hasta la vista vida mia*' she whispered before the Land-Rover disappeared from sight.

★   ★   ★

'If one ignores the ruined fields and the hordes of rescue workers you'd never know there'd been a hurricane,' Philip remarked three days later.

'And to think,' Lisa added with a sigh, 'it's only a week since we were at the beach bungalow.'

Mary's eyes narrowed as she stared

into the distance and Lisa was immediately alert with hope when she followed Mary's gaze and saw a vehicle in the distance approaching the bungalow.

Mary put out her hand and covered Lisa's sympathetically. 'He'll be back as soon as he can dear.'

Lisa smiled her gratitude. 'I know Mary but I can't help watching for him all the time. Before we were married I told him I didn't care if we only had one week as long as we shared it, but it wasn't true. We've had a year and I'm greedy enough to want a hundred more.'

Her eyes were fixed on the still unrecognisable vehicle and she missed the agonised look that passed between Mary and Philip. Philip stood up abruptly at the same time as Lisa recognised the army jeep.

'What does . . . ' she began, turning a pair of panic-stricken eyes on him.

'Relax Lisa. Remember we're just having tea quite normally.'

When the jeep stopped outside the

bungalow Philip and Luis came up onto the veranda.

Luis bowed curtly. '*Buenas tardes Señora Bannerman*,' he said.

'Good afternoon Captain Baldera,' Mary replied coolly. 'Will you have tea?'

'Thank you no. I will keep you a few minutes only.' He turned his icy stare on Lisa who only managed to suppress a shudder with the greatest self control.

'Hello Luis,' she said softly but his face remained impassive. '*Buenas tardes Señora Rodriguez*. I should be obliged if you could tell me where I can find Dr. Rodriguez?'

The silence that followed seemed to last forever. Lisa stirred her cup thoughtfully and then looked up at him, saying easily with a smile, 'Surely you know Luis?'

'I should be obliged if you would tell me Señora.'

Lisa's smile faded. 'He is out attending to casualties of course. Now there are no patients needing surgery he thought he would go out into the

267

villages. I can't tell you exactly which one he's in right now. Is there some emergency?'

He turned abruptly to Philip without bothering to answer Lisa's question. 'Señor Bannerman it seems most of the young men from the village have been missing for several days. Do you know where they have gone?'

'To seek work Captain,' Philip answered without hesitation. 'There is little enough for them on this estate now. I imagine it's the same story on all the other estates.'

'Unfortunately yes Señor,' He bowed again. His gaze rested on Lisa for a moment, chilling her to the marrow and then he said, 'I am sorry to have troubled you Señor Bannerman. *Adios*.'

'*Adios* Captain.'

The three on the veranda watched until the jeep had disappeared into the distance and then of one accord they let out a great sigh.

'Maria!' Mary cried, 'More tea please.' She laughed out loud. 'We certainly need it.'

'Do you think he believed us?' Lisa asked anxiously.

'There's no reason for him to believe otherwise,' Philip replied.

'I do hope so,' Lisa murmured thoughtfully.

★ ★ ★

Lisa revelled in the luxury of a hot shower; in the relatively primitive conditions suffered on Santa Angelina the Bannerman's had somehow managed to endow themselves with the rudiments conducive to comfortable living. Her spirits soared as she towelled herself dry; Miguel would surely be back tonight. He had said he would be gone for no more than a couple of days and already it had been five.

She chose her dress carefully and brushed her hair until it shone like spun gold. Philip had returned from Alhaja some time ago and she surmised both he and Mary would be waiting for her to join them for the customary rum punch before dinner.

On her way she popped into Rowena's room to say goodnight — as she always did when she was at the plantation. The little girl smelled sweet and looked cuddlesome after her bath and as Lisa bent to kiss her soft plump cheek an indiscernible sensation stirred deep within her.

When she entered the room she was a little surprised to see Philip still in the dusty clothes he had been wearing earlier in the day. He and Mary were standing in front of the great fireplace that monopolised the room, their voices low and their heads close together. When they heard her enter their conversation ceased abruptly and they looked up with a guilty start. Lisa's smile faded on her face and a chill of foreboding crept down her spine.

'Something has happened hasn't it? Is it Miguel?'

Philip came across and squeezed her shoulder. 'As far as we know he is perfectly all right.' He paused. 'But there has been trouble in Alhaja today. There was a demonstration outside Pantero's house. It became quite ugly and the soldiers opened fire on the unarmed crowd. Luckily the presence of the Red Cross people prevented more casualties.'

Lisa looked at him anxiously. 'Is that all?'

Philip turned away thoughtfully. 'No,' he said slowly.

'What sparked off this unusual show of bravado was the news that a group of rebels attacked and held the garrison at Punta Grande last night. Punta Grande is a large arsenal and from what I could gather the rebels must have captured enough artillery to flatten Alhaja.'

Lisa sank down onto the sofa, staring sightlessly ahead. 'Oh no.'

'The army was mobilised immediately and the whole island is swarming with jeeps and tanks.'

'So it's come at last,' she said softly to no one in particular.

'We knew it had to Lisa,' Mary said gently. 'The hurricane leaving so many people homeless and without work was just the thing to spark it off.'

The sound of vehicles stopping outside the bungalow made them look at each other with a mixture of hope and fear. Lisa tore across to the window and turned fearfully back to Mary and Philip. 'It's Luis Baldera and at least a dozen men.'

Baldera's voice could already be heard outside snapping orders.

'Let's keep calm,' Philip said tersely as he went across to the door and flung it open.

'Good evening Captain,' Philip said with a heartiness that belied his bloodless face. 'I hear you've had some trouble today.'

Luis Baldera swept into the room followed by two soldiers, carrying rifles. He glanced around. His eyes remained on Lisa. 'You will tell me Señora where I can find your husband.'

'I . . . I don't know. I'm very worried

about him as you can imagine. He has been out attending to casualties for days and now there is this trouble. I'm very concerned.'

'You are wise to be concerned Señora but this act of innocence is no longer convincing. I will ask you once again. Where is he?'

Lisa felt her chin tremble but she met his eyes levelly. 'I don't know,' she answered in all truthfulness.

'Very well. If you do not wish to co-operate you will prepare yourself to accompany me to Alhaja for further questioning.'

'Wait a moment Captain,' Philip broke in, 'Why is Señora Rodriguez being taken into custody?'

'We are questioning any person known to have associated with the enemies of the republic.'

'That is ludicrous,' Mary cried. 'Lisa knows no-one who could possibly be connected with the rebels. We can vouch for that.'

Captain Baldera's lips curved into a

sneer. 'I am not a fool Señora. My hearing is perfect. The name of Miguel Rodriguez is being shouted in the streets as El Salvador.'

Lisa felt the darkness closing in on her; the room swam around her. 'It's not possible!' she cried.

'Can't you see she knows nothing of this?' Philip said angrily.

'We will find out. Please be ready to leave immediately.' He turned his implacable face on Philip. 'You too Señor.'

'This is an abomination,' Philip protested.

'Nevertheless you and your wife and child will accompany me to Alhaja for questioning.'

Lisa snapped out of her daze to look sharply at Philip whose face was suffused with colour. 'What kind of a creature are you Baldera? You know perfectly well el alcazar is no place for women or children. I am quite willing to accompany you although I can tell you now there is nothing I know.'

'Your wife and child will be safe Señor — providing you can prove your loyalty to the republic.' He turned to Mary. 'You will please get the child. We leave in five minutes.'

Mary hesitated, giving an agonised look to her husband who said wearily, 'You'd better do as he says Mary.'

When Mary had gone Luis turned to Lisa, a cruel smile curved his lips. 'When the news of your arrest is made public El Salvador will surely come to the rescue of his fair bride and his best friend.' He walked over to the door, his eyes resting chillingly on Lisa and he said softly, 'But I for one hope it is not too soon.' He turned to Philip. 'Do not think of escape Señor. The house is surrounded and my men have orders to shoot to kill.'

He slammed out of the door followed by his armed guards. Philip went swiftly across to the window. 'He's right. They're all over the place.'

'He's not right about Miguel is he Philip?' she said pleadingly. 'He's not the man they call El Salvador? He can't be or I would have known.'

Philip's eyes rested on her sympathetically. 'I'm afraid so Lisa. He hated it and he thought it would be safer if you didn't know. He got the name when it all started. There were only a handful of them at that time and it was Rafael who said 'They will call you their saviour' and of course it stuck. It wasn't surprising; these people needed some hope to cling to and El Salvador was it. It is more of an ideal than a man. You know he wants no personal glory.'

'Do you think Baldera is right when he says Miguel will try to rescue us? Surely he'll realise it's a trap.'

'I hope so. I know this revolution means a lot to him but I also know we, and especially you, mean more.'

'He didn't want to marry me because of precisely what has happened. I begged him Philip and now look what trouble I've caused — not only to him but to you and Mary too.'

'Don't think like that Lisa. We were

committed years ago, long before you came here and we've always known what risks were involved. As for Miguel I was inclined to believe you shouldn't have married but you couldn't help the way you felt about each other and I know Miguel wouldn't have had it any other way. He's always been happy, but he's also been lonely. Since he married you he hasn't been lonely any more.'

Mary came back leading a dazed and bewildered child. She threw two light coats across to them. 'We'll need these,' she said, her face ashen and drawn.

'What will happen to us when we get there?' Lisa asked as she slipped into her coat.

'I think,' replied Philip heavily, 'it would be better not to think about it.'

★ ★ ★

The army truck bounced along the unlit roads. Lisa and the Bannermans, guarded by two soldiers, sat silently and grim faced at the back. The country was now officially in a state of war but it was all unreal to Lisa. She had not seen any fighting nor any soldiers since it started and she could not imagine Miguel leading the opposition army.

She was afraid, more afraid than she ever imagined she could be but her fear was for Miguel and after praying for his return for so long she now prayed he would stay away. Only now did she understand why he had been so reluctant to marry her; a man who cared about anyone had a weakness at which his enemies could strike.

Rowena dozed fitfully in her mother's arms. The evening was cool but Lisa knew, as she drew her coat around her, the chill she was feeling owed nothing to the weather. Her mind dwelt fearfully on the fate that awaited them at el alcazar; she was aware of the cruelty Luis Baldera was capable of; he had hardly been able to hide his pleasure at the thought of having her as his prisoner.

Suddenly the truck swerved, throwing them to the floor. It bumped along for a few yards and then jerked sharply to a halt. Lisa trembled uncontrollably at the sound of shouting and the staccato firing of machine gun bullets. The two soldiers recovered quickly and leaped from the back of the truck and the firing and shouting started again. Lisa began to get up but Philip pulled her down again.

'Don't move,' he ordered in a terse whisper.

Suddenly the firing stopped and the flap of the truck was thrown back and the four people on the floor looked up fearfully to see two men dressed in an unfamiliar uniform.

'I think we've been rescued,' Philip said in a shaky voice and Rowena began to whimper. Philip jumped down and helped the others out. Lisa looked around her in the gloom and saw that the truck had been driven partly off the road. She peered round the truck and saw shadowy figures running to and fro, shouting warnings and instructions to each other. Seeing anything was difficult on this moonless night but she gasped when her eyes alighted on three figures lying motionless in the road. As she recoiled against the side of the truck she felt Philip's arm go around her shoulder reassuringly.

The noise died down a little and the shadows materialised into men returning to their vehicles. A dozen of them climbed into the truck and it was driven away, leaving two jeeps and a handful of men in the road.

A figure detached itself from the group of men left behind. He stopped briefly by each of the fallen men before straightening up once more. When he came towards them Lisa recognised Miguel and gasped with relief and delight. She tore herself away from the cover of the roadside and began to run towards him, flinging herself into his arms. He held her close for a moment or two and then held her away from him.

'Did they harm you?'

She shook her head and said breathlessly, 'Baldera hoped he would trap you using me as the bait.'

'I know,' he said softly. 'But there is nothing to fear now.'

'But how did you know about us?'

She sensed his smile in the darkness. 'We have friends everywhere.'

'What happened to Baldera and his men?'

'They ran off into the darkness. Come we have little time to spare.'

As he lifted her into the back of one of the jeeps she noticed his face had been left unshaven for several days. He motioned Mary and Philip into the second jeep before climbing in beside Lisa.

'Those men . . . ' she began, looking down at the inert forms in the road.

'There is nothing I can do to help them.' As the jeeps jerked into action he slipped his arm around her shoulder. 'We have a long journey ahead *querida*; try to sleep a little.'

Lisa strolled out into the bright sunshine and stretched luxuriously towards the sky. She gazed around and saw they were in a small village on a flat plateau surrounded by steep forest-covered mountains. She took deep lungfuls of sweet mountain air. Adobe plaster huts with thatched palm roofs had been built in a semi-circle. Curly-horned sheep and dozens of chickens contributed to the cacophany of noise of the village awakening.

The dark and frightening events of the previous evening had already been relegated to the realm of bad dreams.

They had travelled endless miles through the dark unfamiliar country-side. She had dozed spasmodically, only aware of Miguel's comforting presence by her side and the bumping of the jeep on a rough track that she imagined was climbing upwards.

She had been aroused by his arm being withdrawn very gently. She sat up, blood pounding in her ears. They were at el alcazar and there was no escape! She sat back weak with relief when she realised she was no longer Baldera's prisoner.

'Why have we stopped?' she asked dazedly.

He jumped down from the jeep and swung her into his arms. She clasped her arms around his neck, too weary to want to walk. 'We are going to spend the night in this village.'

'Where exactly are we?' she asked as he carried her through the almost total darkness. Somewhere a dog barked and she could hear Rowena's frightened voice echoing her question.

'High up in the mountain. We shall be safe.'

They entered some kind of a building and he set her down on a mat on the floor. 'Aren't the others coming too?'

'They have their own hut,' he replied in the darkness and she recognised his bantering tone as he added, 'but perhaps you would prefer them to be with us.'

Her voice was suddenly choked. 'I've been so worried about you,' she said. 'I bet you haven't had chance to sleep since you left the hospital.'

He crouched down beside her and covering her with a blanket chuckled softly. 'I am fortunate to need only two hours sleep to become refreshed.'

'You, of all people, should know better than that,' she retorted, knowing her sudden sharpness was due more to relief and tiredness than anger.

He lay down beside her and took her hand in his. 'If you continue to contradict me I will wish I had left you to your friend Baldera. He would have tamed you.'

She laughed and turned her head towards him. 'I seem to remember you wanted a chance to do that yourself.'

'In that case I have not done a very good job.'

She snuggled closer and said sleepily. 'You've done a very good job.'

There was no sign of Miguel amongst the incurious villagers but the jeeps were still where they had been left the night before, guarded by men wearing the green battledress of the rebel army.

Lisa caught sight of Mary and Rowena coming out of another hut and she waved to catch their attention. Mary wrinkled her nose. 'I wouldn't say it's exactly five star accommodation,' she looked slyly at Lisa, 'or wouldn't you notice?'

Lisa laughed. 'But it's infinitely better than any Baldera has to offer.'

'Definitely. I never thought I would spend the night sleeping on a palm leaf mat.' She glanced down at her daughter. 'But at least Rowena is enjoying the adventure.'

'Why was Uncle Miguel carrying a gun?' Rowena asked.

'Oh heavens,' Lisa said, 'that is rather a hard question to answer.'

'If we can't change our clothes,' said

Mary, 'we can at least wash. There's a spring behind those huts. When all is said and done I still have this awful addiction to soap and water, despite living in Santa Angelina for twenty years.'

Lisa's eyes anxiously scanned the area. 'A woman brought me some water early this morning. Have you seen Miguel?'

'He's having a pow-wow in the hut with Philip. I thought it would be tactful if I made myself scarce for a while.'

Lisa walked slowly with Mary and Rowena towards the clear spring where several of the village women were washing clothes or utensils. 'I don't suppose they run to an iron,' she said, looking down at her crumpled dress and then with a sigh, 'I wonder where we'll be going from here.'

'I've no doubt they're arranging that now.' Mary dried Rowena's face with her handkerchief and as they walked back Miguel and Philip were just coming out of the hut. Lisa was relieved to see Miguel had shaved.

He smiled down at her. 'Are you ready to leave?'

'Must we go so soon?'

'I must get back to my men as soon as possible.'

'We have to collect our things,' Mary said suddenly, drawing Philip and Rowena away towards the hut they had occupied.

Lisa gazed up at his familiar and beloved face and realised he was suddenly a stranger to her. She shrank away from the knowledge that today he would unhesitatingly take the life of a man whom he would have fought desperately to save a week ago. He was no longer hers alone; until the dreadful fight was won or lost she would have to share him with the thousands of others who were looking to him to lead them to a better life and a more promising future. And her greatest dread of all was the fear that he would never be the same again.

Her new-found revelation left her shy. 'I can't get used to seeing you like this,' she said.

His eyes did not leave hers for a moment. 'I don't want you to get used to seeing me like this. I am praying it will soon be over and I can return to the work I was trained to do.'

She looked away, knowing every moment with him was precious, yet aware she was wasting them. He took both her hands in his saying, 'You know I love you, don't you Lisa? And all I want is to return to our life together?'

She looked at him again and smiled, 'Yes I do know Miguel and I love you too, very much.'

'We're ready,' Philip announced, coming out of the hut, followed by his wife and daughter.

Lisa tore her hand from his. 'I'll just get my coat,' she said as she turned and ran towards the hut.

The journey down the mountains was an experience Lisa was never likely to forget. The track they followed seemed hardly fit for goats let alone jeeps. A dewy umbrella of mountain ferns anointed them as they passed beneath and it was not long before they began to feel damp and uncomfortable. But the mountain slopes possessed a wild beauty all their own. Magnificent trees stood so close together there was hardly room for a man to pass between, while colourful birds swooped through the branches shrieking excitedly to one another. Timid iguanas withdrew into the forests as the jeeps intruded into the solitude of their mountain retreat and wherever Lisa turned wild orchids clung in riotous profusion to the trees.

As they passed through a narrow gorge Lisa thought she had never seen a more beautiful sight than that of a waterfall, its droplets multi-hued in the sunlight as it cascaded with a deafening roar down the valley and fragmented into a billowing cloud of spray.

At last the track widened and the terrain became less hilly. Through the trees Lisa frequently caught sight of the silvery reflection of sun on sea. At this part of the island the mountains dropped almost directly into the sea and when the land levelled off she found they were on a rough road running parallel with the sea. The area seemed uninhabited; they had not seen human life since leaving the village. She wondered where Miguel was taking them, but was somehow reluctant to ask.

The jeeps swung off the road and went along the beach itself for a way and when Lisa caught sight of a fishing boat bobbing gently on the water she felt her first pricking of fear.

Miguel jumped down the moment the jeep stopped on the edge of the sands and before she could say anything he swung her down beside him. 'I must leave you for a little while *querida*.'

She switched her alarm-filled gaze from the boat back to him. 'Are we to go aboard?'

'Yes. Orlando will take good care of you.' He turned to Philip. 'Get Mary and Rowena on board Philip. Lisa will follow in a minute.'

'Where are we going?' she asked warily.

'Orlando will take you as far as Jamaica. From there you can fly to New York and then London.'

'No!' The word was wrung from her. Mary who was already in the water wading towards the boat turned in alarm and was then hurried on by Philip who was carrying Rowena.

'Please Lisa, don't make it more difficult for me. You must go. Surely you must realise it after last night.'

Lisa began to struggle out of his grasp, tears streaming down her face. 'I won't go!' she cried. 'I won't go. If I leave the island now I'll never see you again!'

He caught her wrists and held them tightly to him. 'You must see reason. While you are here I shall worry about you and if I worry about you I cannot concentrate on the job in hand. I am responsible for thousands of lives; just as I am responsible for the patient on the operating table. If I were working at the hospital you would not want me to be worried about you, would you?'

'I can't leave you. Please don't make me,' she sobbed. 'I don't care how bad living conditions are as long as I can stay.'

'You must go *amor mio* and now. There are coastal patrols and we have been lucky so far. You cannot do anything while you are here but if you go to America and England you can tell our story to the world press. Let them know what we are really fighting for; the truth and not just Pantero's version.' She clung on to him tightly. 'It is a vitally important job I am entrusting you with. Will you do it?'

She pulled away from him at last. 'I have no choice,' she said in a dull voice.

Gently he wiped the tears away from her face with the tips of his fingers. 'By the time you reach London — or even New York — this may be over and I want you to promise me you will catch the first boat back.'

She smiled at him through her tears. 'It would take an army bigger than the American and British combined to stop me.'

'*Patrullar!*'

Lisa looked up sharply to see an army jeep approaching in the distance. Miguel stooped briefly to kiss her lips before swinging her into his arms and wading into the water. Philip caught her as Miguel put her over the side but she still did not let go of him. As he kissed her hand he said, 'This has been the happiest year of my life.'

The engine spluttered into life and the boat began to move away. She still kept a desperate hold of his hand. As it slid from her grasp her tears began to fall anew and over the throbbing of the engine she heard him shout 'I shall be waiting.'

11

Lisa stared down into the little Kensington side street. It was already dark; everyone was hurrying home. Home to their husbands and sweethearts. Home to someone. It was already snowing in the country and the forecast was snow for London too. Lisa shivered; she hadn't been able to get warm since leaving Santa Angelina. And how many years had that been? Only three months — hardly that really.

She still lay awake nights yearning for the familiar chirping of the cicadas instead of the incessant roar of the traffic below her window and she still reached out for Miguel's comforting presence beside her when she awoke in the middle of the night.

Her lips curved into an involuntary smile at the memory of Christmas. Philip, Mary and herself eating turkey and plum pudding in the hotel dining room, their paper hats at odds with the expressions of their faces. Only Rowena was gay, revelling in the unique experience of Christmas in London and all it had to offer.

Now it was January and in Santa Angelina the sun would be shining; shining on the yellow and scarlet poinsettia and please God it would be shining on Miguel too.

Three months and no real news from Santa Angelina. The civil war was still raging and confusion reigned. Communications had been cut, journalists expelled and no one knew which side, if any, was winning.

For three months Lisa lived only to read the latest edition of the newspaper or hear the news reports on the radio. The conflict that had at first filled the front page of every newspaper had eventually been relegated to an inner page and gradually shortening paragraphs.

Philip haunted the news agencies but

their correspondents had not been allowed to land on the island and were now biding their time in Jamaica, until the battle was won and they were invited to meet the victor.

Through all the agonised weeks of waiting Lisa was continually haunted by morbid dreams of Miguel lying broken and bleeding in el alcazar, Miguel delirious with fever, and Miguel lying mortally wounded in some village square.

She picked up her room key and went along the corridor to the Bannermans' room. Mary looked up from her knitting and smiled. 'I thought you'd be along. You must have an instinct for news bulletins by now.' She studied her face and frowned. 'You don't look well dear.'

Lisa sat down next to Philip who was immersed in his newspaper. He was making the most of his enforced exile by relaxing as he never could when he had the plantation to run. 'I'm well,' she answered, 'just worried. I can't pretend otherwise.'

'I know dear, but you should see a doctor you know. Whatever happens you must plan for the future.'

Lisa stared into space. 'I don't need a doctor to tell me what I already know Mary.'

'Well think how pleased Miguel will be when he learns he's going to be a father.'

'I wish I could be sure he will know.'

Philip refolded his paper. 'Miguel has a very stubborn streak Lisa. If he says he'll be waiting when you go back, he certainly will.'

Lisa laughed then. 'I wish I had your optimism. But we don't even know if they escaped the patrol when we left the island.'

'Oh I'm sure they did,' Philip replied thoughtfully. 'Otherwise the revolution would have folded up before now.'

'Even when he told me he was involved with the rebels,' Lisa said, miserably contemplating the toe of her shoe. 'I didn't really believe it was as anything more than a doctor.'

'Probably it's a bit of both,' Mary said comfortingly. 'He always could do the work of ten men. I only wish I had his stamina and energy. You must try to stop worrying so much Lisa. He's probably safe in some hide-out in the hills, organising the battles with Rafael and attending to the sick and wounded. He's far too valuable to them to risk his life in the line of fire.'

Rowena came out of the bedroom. 'Oh goody,' she cried when she saw Lisa, 'Will you read to me from my new book.'

'Later,' Lisa promised, 'after we've heard the news report.'

Rowena's face became sulky. 'But you're always listening to the radio,' she complained.

Mary leaned over and switched on. The room was filled with music. 'One thing we have to be grateful for and that is sitting this thing out in comfort.'

'And I can pop around the corner for my tobacco instead of having it sent,' added Philip.

But Lisa knew they longed to be back in Santa Angelina as much as she did.

Mary sighed. 'I suppose we shall have to sit through a lot of dreary reports about the price of coal and the useless questions asked in Parliament today.' Her face softened.

'Well as least it's democracy and that's what it's all about.'

Lisa tensed as she always did when she heard the pips. She knew the routine — fifteen minutes of hopeful tension as the newscaster touched on every subject except the one they were desperate to hear and then the disappointment until the next time when the whole process would be repeated.

At the beginning the news had been all about the little republic and its struggle. On her arrival in New York Lisa had been frightened at the sight of a hundred reporters and photographers who were waiting at the airport. Through mists of fatigue and worry she had told her story; Philip too. The same happened in London, only the reception was less feverish than in New York but the interest was greater because the wife of the leader of the revolution was British. The name of Miguel Rodriguez known as El Savador was on every newspaper hoarding and on every newscaster's lips. Wherever she went there was interest; reporters begged interviews with her and women journalists wanted her views on cooking and the latest fashions. In a way Lisa was glad — it kept her busy, and she needed to be kept busy.

She hardly recognised the man who figured so prominently in the news. Lisa had tried hard to put over his sincerity and the reasons why he abandoned a successful career in the United States to return to the country of his birth, but the newspapers had made him out to be a saint. She often wondered if the man fighting oppression was the same man she first met in the garden of La Casa des flores and the man who had kissed her so tenderly.

And at the back of her mind she wondered — should he live through it all — if he would ever be that man again. She knew, should the rebels win, the country would insist on having him as the new president and in order to build up confidence in the new regime he would have no option but to accept.

Mary and Lisa sat, eyes glued to the radio, while Philip puffed placidly on his pipe. Suddenly they all tensed, straining forward although the voice came over loud and clear.

'The revolution in Santa Angelina is over,' he announced and Lisa felt her hands tighten on the arm of her chair. 'It was officially announced today in Alhaja de mar, the capital of Santa Angelina, that the victorious revolutionary army took the capital — the last stronghold of the army — three days ago.'

Lisa exchanged triumphant looks with Philip and Mary before retaining her attention to the radio. Her knuckles were white from gripping the arm of the chair. 'Conditions on the island,' he continued, 'are still in a state of chaos but it has been confirmed that Señor Rafael Jeron has been appointed president of the republic. Señor Jeron, a lawyer, was second in command to Dr. Miguel Rodriguez known as El Salvador. There is no news of the fate of Dr. Rodriguez or of the deposed President Pantero.

'It is announced from Buckingham Palace that Her Majesty the Queen will visit Thailand in the autumn . . . '

Philip leaned over and switched off the radio. There was absolute silence in the room for a moment before he said, 'The whole island must be chaotic. Because there's no news of him doesn't mean to say . . . '

'He's dead,' Lisa said woodenly.

'There's no reason to believe that dear,' Mary said soothingly. 'In a few days the position will become much clearer.'

'He is dead,' she repeated. 'If he was alive he would be president now.

Outside of Santa Angelina Rafael's name has hardly been mentioned. Miguel was the leader. Who else would they have if he were alive.'

'We still can't be sure . . . ' Mary said.

Lisa looked at her. 'I'm sure. I knew I'd never see him again. I just knew it . . . '

She jumped to her feet and ran out of the room. Mary made to follow her but Philip put a restaining arm on hers, 'Let her alone for a while,' he said. 'She'll have to come to terms with it in her own way. Whatever we say we know she's right.'

* ★ ★

She stared ahead into the darkness. She didn't mind the darkness; it was her friend. From now on she would live in darkness and never see the sun.

It had happened as she always knew it would. She had loved him too much. No person should love another as she had loved him. Yes she had known. Not just for three months but from that moment on the beach when he had told her of his involvement with the rebels.

We had a year together, she thought. A year. It was nothing. They had only just begun to know each other, only just begun to love. Now it was over before it had even begun. Now she would have to learn to live without him by her side and she wondered how she could attempt the impossible. She wondered what it was going to be like never to have him smile at her again, have his arms crush her close or feel his lips caress hers.

The struggle he had given his heart to had taken his life and in a month his name wouldn't even be remembered; he was only another casualty of the war and that to Lisa was the greatest tragedy. The revolution did not need Miguel Rodriguez — there was always someone ready to lead an insurrection — and she did.

She didn't even turn when the door

opened and the light flashed on. 'Lisa you haven't had any dinner.'

'I don't want any food thank you Mary.'

Mary came across the room and knelt down by her side. 'We can understand how you feel but you must be sensible. There are certain realities you have to face. You can't neglect yourself now, however wretched you feel.'

Lisa wondered how she would feel once the child was born. She supposed she would love him, especially if he looked like Miguel but just now she felt nothing. And she resented not being able to indulge in her own misery.

'You'll have to decide what you're going to do,' Mary continued. 'Are you going to stay in England with your aunts and have the baby here?'

'No. I'm going back to Santa Angelina. They'll need teachers and I want my child to be born there.' She had to go back, to continue what Miguel had started. 'Tomorrow there

305

will be a better life for him,' he had said. It was what he had fought for.

'We're going back too.' Lisa looked at her for the first time. 'Philip will only be happy when he's back there and to be truthful so will I. He's finished with planting sugar for his own pocket — he's made quite a lot of money. Now he wants to join the education programme once it gets going, probably teaching the scientific side of sugar cane planting. He's going to try and get us on the first flight to New York. From there we should be able to get a boat.'

'I shall be ready.'

Mary stood up to go and looked at Lisa for a moment. 'There's nothing definite; we can still hope.' When she didn't reply she said, 'Philip has known him for more than thirty years, since he was a little boy. We've both followed his progress with a great deal of pride, so you're not alone in this dear. And there's always a home for you with us.'

Lisa smiled at her. 'I know Mary and thank you.'

★ ★ ★

It was the second time Lisa had approached Santa Angelina by boat. The first time she had been bubbling over with enthusiasm, anticipating her future on the island. This time there was no gaiety in her manner as the boat entered the bay of Alhaja de mar.

Life, she could see, was already returning to normal. Fishing boats and inter-island schooners were moored in the harbour once again while their skippers went about their business ashore. There was nothing left of the ramshackle clapboard of buildings along the wharf except for mounds of charred wood.

The boat tied up at the wharf and Lisa saw the president's limousine was standing there, just as it had been on that other occasion. The man who stood beside it was not Luis Baldera in the khaki and red uniform of Pantero's Personal Guard but another man in the green uniform of the new army.

'I shall be waiting,' he had said. His

voice echoed in her ears. She had always feared the worst but hope didn't really die until that moment and she lay her head on her arms resting on the rail and was able to cry at last.

She felt a hand on her arm and looked up to find Philip standing beside her. 'It's time to go ashore,' he said gently.

The man waiting by the limousine looked vaguely familiar and when they approached him Lisa realised he had been a worker on Philip's estate. He smiled broadly when he saw them. 'Welcome back Señor and Señoras.'

'Thank you José,' Philip replied. 'Surely you were not expecting us?'

'No Señor, but I have orders from Señor Jeron to meet every boat that arrives. They have been arriving frequently over the past two days. The island is bursting at the seams with journalists and businessmen wanting to invest their money.'

Philip turned back to the women. 'It's just as well he's here to meet us,' he said, 'we'd better pay our respects to Jeron first and find out if our bungalow is still there.'

Lisa hesitated, wanting to ask José if he knew what had happened to Miguel, but fear held her back; she wasn't sure she could face the knowledge just yet.

On the short journey from the harbour to the square the evidence of three months desperate fighting was very apparent. Where tall buildings had crowded the narrow roads there was only rubble-strewn waste land. An odd building was still precariously upright but these were already being bulldozed. Here and there stood a piece of furniture, an iron bedstead, a painting of the madonna, hurriedly left behind in the rush for safety.

'Just as well,' Philip commented. 'Now they can build decent and sanitary homes.'

Barbed wire barricades and walls of sandbags still stood in la plaza which was now teeming with the military and the Red Cross people who had never left after the hurricane. Lisa could not look at the hospital as they passed, although she did notice the large gaping holes in its wall. One day the ache in her heart would fade enough to allow her to be proud of marrying a hero, to rejoice in the newfound prosperity that would surely come to her adoptive country, and to take pride in the small part she would play.

The wall surrounding La Casa des flores had been completely demolished by mortar fire and the courtyard was crowded with jeeps and military trucks. As she passed into the house Lisa recognised many of the men who once wore shabby and tattered clothes and now proudly wore the uniform of the new army. Inside the house the hall was filled with soldiers and in the middle Rafael was being interviewed by a group of journalists.

Lisa with the others waited by the door. 'During the next few months,' Rafael was telling the journalists, 'most of the soldiers you see will be demobilised and returned to civilian duties so that the task of rebuilding the country can be tackled without delay.'

He is the perfect man for the job, Lisa thought without bitterness, as she watched him. Already he might have been president for years, so well did he suit the position. He was a natural leader. Miguel would have hated all this attention, she realised, while Rafael basked in it. Perhaps fate had ordained the right man should survive.

'We are immediately embarking on a full programme of house building. We have been very fortunate to be offered materials and expert help from several countries. Schools and hotels are next on the list of priorities. Within a year education will be compulsory for all children up to the age of fourteen and it is hoped to extend this limit as our school building plan is expanded. We shall certainly be able to pay all our debts in time.' He paused to listen to a question being put to him. 'We estimate that the country will be ready to choose its own government in two years time. By then we will have repaired the damage done by the hurricane and the war. There will certainly be a free election and anyone will be welcome to stand as a candidate.' He caught sight of Lisa and Philip and said hurriedly, 'That will be all the questions for now gentlemen.'

He hurried across to them, shaking Philip's hand vigorously. 'Welcome back my friend.'

'We're glad to be back Rafael and congratulations. We stopped by to find out if our bungalow is still standing.'

'It is, but it has been used to house homeless families up until now. You are welcome to stay here until it is free again.'

'We wouldn't dream of it Rafael,' Mary cut in. 'I've no doubt we can squeeze in until they are able to move out.'

He turned smilingly to Lisa and grasped her hands in his. 'How can we ever thank you for being such a good ambassadress for our country. All the aid we are now receiving is because you pleaded our case so well and aroused the world's support and sympathy for our struggle.'

Lisa was embarrassed. 'It was nothing,' she said in a choked voice.

'That is open to dispute.' His face became more serious. 'It is a great pity Miguel is unable to be here to meet you, but it was unavoidable. I am sure you will understand how bad things have been here. The casualties have been very heavy . . . '

Lisa tore her hands from his grasp and in a voice thick with emotion she said 'Excuse me Rafael,' and pushed past him and through the crowds of journalists still thronging the hall.

Unconsciously she fled in the direction of the veranda and she heard Rafael say in a grave voice, 'It has been trying for her too. We have all had to make sacrifices.'

She paused on the deserted veranda taking in deep gulps of air. Rafael was right, of course, she had made a sacrifice. A sacrifice made by countless other women on the island. And even now all those women would be learning to live with their loss. She must learn to accept it, she thought. It was her tragedy and no one else's.

All over the island at this very moment the fields were being cleared ready for a new crop of sugar. In a year the fields would once again be filled with the tall green cane swaying in the wind. Life would go on . . .

She went down the veranda steps marvelling that the garden showed no signs of the havoc that reigned all over the rest of the island. The garden that had given her so much consolation during her first days in Santa Angelina was as colourful and luxuriant as ever. She needed that comfort again now.

She sank down on the same iron seat where she had been sitting when she first set eyes on him. Everywhere was the same fragrance of the sweet frangipani blossom. When she had first arrived she had picked some of the pale pink and red star-shaped flowers for her room, only to find they had faded almost immediately she had picked them.

A green-breasted humming bird fluttered in the tree. She wondered if it were the same one she had watched on that fateful day. Or perhaps it was a descendant. Life went on . . .

Someone was coming down the path from the house. Lisa sighed. Philip and Mary must want to go home. She was aware she was fast becoming a trial to them. She would have to apologise for the last time and then lock her grief away where it could not be seen by the outside world.

The footsteps stopped beside her and unwillingly she looked up, the apology on her lips. But no words came.

'Say something *querida* even if it is only hello.'

In an instant she was on her feet and in his arms. He held her close, burying his face in the silky softness of her hair.

'I thought you were dead,' she managed to say after a while.

He held her at arms length. 'I told you I would be waiting. I would have come to meet you if I had known when you were coming. Rafael has only just sent word of your arrival. I am so happy to have you back Lisa. Every day without you was like a month.'

She smiled up at him. 'It was for me too. The worst part was not knowing. When we heard Rafael was president we assumed the worst.' She gazed at his face, without so much as a scratch. The dark days were over. He was with her again, dressed as a civilian and not in the hateful green uniform that had looked so alien on him. 'I still dare not believe you're safe.'

'Will this convince you?' He bent his head and their lips met. Lisa clung onto him with the desperate fear that he would disappear again. When they parted at last he drew her down beside him on the seat. 'You knew, surely, I would never accept the presidency? It was never meant to be that way. I am no politician. As soon as the fighting was over I returned to the hospital and I have been working there day and night ever since. Rafael is far more qualified to be president than I. He is an articulate man of great charm — a natural politician.'

'I know, but I still believed the people would have no one else.'

'You give me too much credit. I played only a small part. Rafael has many good men from which to choose his government.'

'What has happened to Pantero and Inés?' she asked hesitatingly.

'They are safe. Pantero had already planned his escape in the event of losing and he and Inés accompanied by Baldera left as soon as we captured Alhaja. I believe they are in the Bahamas now. Pantero provided for the eventuality and he will be able to enjoy a luxurious life as a deposed dictator. Fortunately he had to leave behind all the valuable paintings and statues he bought with our money. They will be sold to provide funds for all we need to do.

'And now he is no longer an army officer perhaps Inés will have a good influence on Baldera. I think she always had a soft spot for him but he was always too busy stamping on people to notice women.'

'I'm glad they've escaped, especially Inés. She will be much happier now, I'm sure.'

Miguel turned her face towards his with one finger under her chin. 'And now there are no shadows looming over us Lisa. Next year there will be a brand new hospital outside Alhaja and we will have our own house. Just the two of us . . . '

He bent to kiss her again, but she shook her head gravely. 'The three of us,' she said, suppressing a smile.

She was rewarded by the surprise and then pleasure that passed across his face. 'That makes everything doubly marvellous. For a moment I was afraid you wanted to stay at the convent with the nuns.'

With a laugh she said, 'If there's one place I certainly don't belong it's a convent!' And she slipped her arms around his neck, drawing his face down to her own.

THE END

Other titles in the
Linford Romance Library:

TUDOR STAR

Sara Judge

Meg Dawlish becomes companion to Lady Penelope Rich whom she loves and admires. Her mistress, unhappily married, meets the two loves of her life — Sir Philip Sidney, and Sir Charles Blount . . . Meg partakes in the excitement of the Accession Day Tilts and visits the house of the Earl of Essex . . . When Meg falls in love she has to decide whether to leave her mistress and life at court, and follow her lover to the wilds of Shropshire.

SAY IT WITH FLOWERS

Chrissie Loveday

Daisy Jones has abandoned her hectic London life for a more peaceful existence in her old home town. Taking on a florist business is another huge gamble, but she loves it and the people she meets. Her new life brings a new love and her life looks set for happiness . . . until the complications set in. Nothing is quite what it seems and she sets off on an emotional roller coaster. Who said life in a small town is peaceful?